The Behavioral Disordered

By: Jason D'Antonio

for Mattt

Chapter 1

Sunnyslope, Illinois

As I woke up to my phone alarm going off, I felt the usual wave of anxiety come over me. It was the fall of 2011, my senior year had just started a few weeks earlier, and just like most days, I was late for school. Even though I was still exhausted from the restless sleep, I quickly shot out of bed, got ready as fast as I could, and raced off to school on my skateboard. As I skated, I looked at my phone to check the time, hoping to at least get there before the second period started. It was eight-thirteen a.m., and school began at seven forty-five. I started skating faster, but the quicker my pace, the more and more anxious I got. My heart started racing, and I began to shake as I obsessed over the intrusive thoughts about how everything in my life was gonna change next year after I graduated from high school.

Between the anxiety of rushing to avoid being late and me having to enter the real world soon even though I didn't feel ready, it seemed as if I was going to have another bad day. Given how often I had days like this one, I knew by now that I just needed to be alone to clear my head and find a way to distract myself.

I thought about calling one of my best friends, particularly my friend Sweetheart. She was always there when I needed her. I could talk to some of my guy friends about a lot, but sometimes it felt weird talking about certain things. When it came to Sweetheart, though, I could tell her anything. Sweetheart was my only female friend, and I had noticed her back during our freshman year. Sweetheart was a blonde-haired girl with blue eyes and a smile that I could only describe as a natural antidepressant. She was a very gentle, humble, sweet, sensitive, yet assertive girl, who didn't take disrespect from anybody, which is why I gave her the nickname. I knew Sweetheart never ditched class, but I also knew if I told her that I needed her, she would come to me. I didn't want her to get into trouble for missing school, though. So I decided not to bother her or any of the rest of my friends.

No! They're all busy. And I have to learn how to deal with problems on my own, I told myself.

With my mind still going crazy, I decided to just ditch school and take the day off. In the back of my mind, I knew that I would get into trouble when my dean found out, and I also knew my Ma would be angry about it when she heard, although in the negative state I was in and with my nerves about being around all of those people, I really didn't care about the consequences at the moment. I just needed to get my mind off of all the uncertainty and change because I was having a really severe anxiety attack.

I stopped and thought quickly as the fight, flight, or freeze response kicked in. I closed my eyes and tried to relax, but I couldn't seem to catch my breath, and the thoughts kept coming uncontrollably. I felt more and more anxious by the second, but then it hit me. A place where I could go have some fun and be alone. Somewhere I knew no one else would be at this time on a weekday. I smiled and instantly felt a slight relief, as I instinctively jumped back on my skateboard and skated off towards the skatepark.

I was diagnosed with social anxiety disorder, obsessive-compulsive disorder, post traumatic stress disorder, and severe depression. With the diagnosis, my difficulty dealing with change and everyday stress made more sense. I was often daydreaming or writing, and I kept to myself. I rarely talked to people except those I was really close to. Those I felt comfortable enough to open up to more. Yet, even when it came to my family and friends, I sometimes came off as cold or distant since I was short and unresponsive. It really bothered me when I could tell I had hurt someone's feelings or when I came across as suddenly mean for no reason, but I was usually too anxious to say I was sorry.

It also bothered me how often I was misjudged. I was often the quiet kid who sat alone in the corner because I struggled to form connections with people, and usually everybody tends to stay away from people like us. One of the many problems with having social anxiety disorder is the constant fear of saying the wrong thing. I was shown at an early age that when you say the wrong thing, you'll get hit, screamed at, or worse. A lot of people like to target the quiet loner until they decide to stand up for themselves, and then they look at us like we are the bad guys.

It also makes forming relationships nearly impossible. Most of my friends were actually friends with my older brother first, until I eventually became close with them as well. I didn't make any friends of my own until I reached sixth and seventh grade, and the only reason that happened was the smaller classes I was put in during middle school. Otherwise, because I was always so quiet, I probably never would've made friends of my own. I was able to get to know people quickly by constantly listening and watching them, but the relationships were mostly one-sided, given the other person couldn't get to know me as easily. I always had an extreme fear of losing someone important to me, and I often imagined saying the wrong thing or disagreeing with someone, just to have that person who meant the world to me end up hating me.

I think the worst part of social anxiety disorder, though, is the opportunities and good times you miss out on. Sometimes I feel like a ghost just watching life unfold, unable to actually affect anything around me. It's almost impossible not to live in the past, or the future when you can't live in the present. So, as I skated

4

through town towards the skatepark, trying to escape my thoughts, I noticed how my thoughts adapted to my surroundings, and it felt like no matter how fast I skated, I couldn't lose them, and I started thinking about where I grew up.

I grew up living with my brothers, my Ma, my grandparents, and my aunt. Me and my friends and family all lived in a small town called Sunnyslope. Sunnyslope is a suburb of Chicago, Illinois, about eighteen miles outside of the city. The town is mostly a middle-class neighborhood, though there are some low-income and some very wealthy households, depending on how far north or south you go.

Our family all worked at a local church. On Sundays, the church provided lunch for everyone who attended the service, and my family prepared the meals each week. The church also had a boxing club in the basement where kids could learn the basics of boxing. The boxing club was organized in an attempt to keep kids from selling drugs and joining gangs. Our Ma, aunt, and grandparents handled the kitchen, and we three boys were in charge of the Gym called THR33 J's BOXING CLUB, led by my older brother Jon.

Sunnyslope was a nice town, but over the years, that began to change. It started with a heroin epidemic. Most of the public was unaware at first, but teenagers began selling and doing the drugs, and it wasn't long before kids began overdosing and, eventually, dying. I didn't know which part of town I couldn't stand the most.

When I finally arrived at the skatepark, I immediately started doing any tricks I could. Since I had struggled to focus on the present. I noticed that most people I have met often misunderstand obsessive-compulsive disorder. A lot of people think that someone with OCD just cleans a lot or has to arrange everything a certain way. While sometimes that's true, what the average person doesn't realize is the other ways it affects you.

In my case, I constantly dealt with intrusive thoughts and compulsions. Intrusive thoughts are uncontrollable thoughts or images that constantly pop up into my head without warning. Imagine the worst things you can do. Horrible things that you know are wrong. Then imagine thoughts and mental pictures of those things possessing you all day every day. My imagination is what made me late for school more often than not. I was a rebellious teenager, struggling with everyday things that seemed to come more naturally to everyone else.

On top of that, I also have compulsive behaviors, such as washing or disinfecting my hands every time I touch something or constantly looking for the numbers 13, 33, 3, and 7. When you don't feel like you're in complete control of your actions, and you constantly get immoral, scary, and negative thoughts that you then obsess over, you feel like you're destined to lose control of yourself and become a monster. I'm a loner, not just because my social anxiety made it hard to talk to people, or because my PTSD made me anxious around strangers, crowds, and unfamiliar places, or because my depression often made me feel sad and nihilistic and I needed time to myself.

One of the main reasons I kept to myself is that I was always terrified that I was dangerous, and that I was gonna hurt someone. I thought the evilest people throughout history started with these thoughts and compulsions, and I didn't want to hurt anyone or become a bad person. This is why I was always obsessed with superheroes. I wanted to live in a world where the good guys win since I had seen that in real life that didn't happen as often as I expected, and I also thought that if I could become a hero, it would prevent me from becoming a villain.

I shook my head forcefully and came back to reality as I tried to get all the bad thoughts out of my head, and I continued skating. This eventually worked, and I was able to temporarily get the negative thoughts out of my head. I fell a few times, getting angrier every time I failed, but after about seven tries, I finally landed the trick, and the amount of happiness I felt was overwhelming. I wasn't used to being that happy or excited, so I looked around the skatepark uncomfortably to make sure I was still alone, which thankfully I still was. That was the best part about skateboarding. Finally landing that trick you've been working on all day and feeling accomplished.

After a couple of hours of calming myself down, I called my older brother, Jon, for a ride. I'm the middle one, in between Jon and my younger brother, Jeff. Jon, two years older than me and six years older than Jeff, was the typical older brother who always had way too much weight put on his shoulders and always instinctively looked out for all of his friends and family. Jon had always tried to be the most modest of us three brothers and even with most of our friends. He was one of the oldest members of the group, and I think he knew he set the example for the rest of us. I thought that Jon was a little too nice at times, though. He, just like my Ma, tended to care about other people too much and not care about himself enough.

Jon was always a lot more social than me. We often disagreed and argued over our different views and opinions on everything, and even though he was more mature than Jeff and me, he too did get into his fair share of trouble, especially in his adolescence. This caught up with him when he became an adult, and he ended up dropping out of high school because he had ditched so often with Zero, one of his best friends, and another one of his friends, Greg. He would have had to repeat his entire senior year. It took some time, but with a little help, Jon managed to catch up after being behind due to his past mistakes.

I always kinda felt like the black sheep since Jon and Jeff were both very popular around Sunnyslope. Most of the guys around either respected or feared them, and they didn't struggle with girls as much as I did. Most people only knew who I was because of my brothers. I even looked different from them. We are Irish and Italian, and they both had Italian features, with their black hair and brown eyes just like my parents had, while I had always had Irish features, with my brown hair and green eyes. I was always proud that my brothers were so popular and respected, but I also daydreamed about a time when I would know what that was like myself.

As Jon pulled up to get me, Jeff got out of the car and skated towards the skatepark.

"What's up, Jay?" Jeff nodded to me, skating faster and faster towards the entrance of the skatepark. I forced a smile and nodded to him as he passed me. I could tell he was excited, his tongue was hanging out and flapping in the wind just like Michael Jordan's did when he played basketball. I heard him scream a swear word, and I turned around, surprised for a second, and laughed slightly when I saw him get up from the ground, shake his head, then kick the rock that clearly made him fall. So, I made sure he got into the skatepark before getting into the car.

Being the youngest, Jeff was naturally the biggest troublemaker, mainly because his big brothers and all of our friends were always there to look out for him and get him out of any trouble he got himself into. Jeff was now twelve, but back when we first moved to Sunnyslope, he was only seven years old. He may have had the same features as Jon, but his personality was completely different. He was a very mischievous and childish teenager, who took more risks than he should. While Jon was at times a little too nice, Jeff in contrast, had a habit of not being nice enough. Jon was the heart that often put everyone else first, while Jeff was the brain and often put only himself and the people he cared about first. Meanwhile, I think I was kind of a combination of both, not as intelligent as Jeff but not as humble as Jon.

Even though he was the youngest, Jeff was always the best skateboarder of the three of us, and he attempted tricks that even Jon and I thought were too risky. Jeff was a handful, but he was also the coolest little brother you could've asked for. He made every day a good time. He would pull pranks and constantly do and say funny things. Jeff also loved playing video games and he often got into trouble with our Ma for screaming swear words whenever he lost. Jeff had his first out-of-school suspension in third grade after all three of us and a couple of friends broke into my old middle school on a Sunday so we could skate. Not only did he get suspended, but he also got arrested. Picking up all three of her sons from the police station, one of which was still in elementary school, was something our Ma wasn't too happy about.

When Jon picked me up, I thought I seemed fine on the outside, but apparently I didn't.

"Are you okay?" asked Jon

"Yeah," I said, knowing I was being short with him but trying not to take my day out on him.

"You seem pissed off," he said casually

"I'm fine. I'm just mad because I broke my skateboard," I said as I continued trying not to be irritable towards him, but I couldn't help it. I was now back to my usual slightly less level of anxiety, just in time for the depression to take over.

"Why weren't you in school?" Jon asked.

"Do you wanna stop uptown by Renegades, so I could get a new skateboard?" I asked, completely ignoring his question. I knew he meant well, and he was just trying to help me learn from his mistakes, but I didn't really want to talk to him about what was going on. We rarely saw eye to eye, and I always felt he was very critical about everything I did. We were good at working together and helping when it came to other people's problems, but we never could handle our own problems together. I guess being almost exact opposites was a good thing sometimes, considering we would be able to challenge the other one's decisions and teach each other different point of views. This caused a lot of tension, but, on occasion, proved helpful for both of us.

After I got my new board, the two of us headed home. On the way home, as we drove through town down Thirteenth Street, we passed a bar called The Chirish Pub, a place we had been with our friends countless times throughout our childhood to play pool. As we drove by, I thought I saw our old friend Zero, who we hadn't seen in a few years. I knew it had to be him by the purple and black striped hoodie. He must have recognized Jon's car, and waved us down, trying to get us to stop and say hello.

"I think that was Zero," said Jon

"Yeah, it was," I replied, annoyed and brooding.

"Should we go say hi?" Jon asked

"You can, but I'm not," I said, now aggravated. I had just started to calm down a little bit, and seeing Zero now might make me have another anxiety attack.

"Come on... it's Zero!" Jon pleaded

"Not the Zero we knew," I responded, feeling even sadder than I had a minute earlier. I felt a sharp pain in my stomach and struggled to catch my breath. I felt nihilistic just thinking about what I had just said.

"Fine, I'll be right back," Jon finished with a slight nod and a disappointed look on his face.

As he pulled into a parking spot, I couldn't tell if the disappointed look on his face was because of me or Zero, but since he could tell I was having a rough day, I assumed he was trying to be understanding. He knew exactly why I was so cold towards our friend, and part of him felt the same way I did. It was hard for me to get close to people and trust others. I also think I was way too sensitive most of the time. This could make me unwilling to give second chances, which I felt was often necessary, but this time it would come back to haunt me.

I watched from a distance as Jon approached Zero, and Zero rushed towards Jon excitedly. The two shook hands and hugged. I could tell the two of them exchanged pleasantries to catch up. Before we drifted apart from Zero, Zero had been like an older brother to me and Jeff, and we had looked up to him as much as we looked up to Jon. Zero had also always looked out for the two of us, especially since he never had any younger brothers of his own, and he and Jon were inseparable. I sat back in the car and got lost thinking about everything that had happened since we and Zero drifted apart. I actually smiled and felt happy for a few minutes as I remembered when we first met him back in 2005, the summer right before I started sixth grade.

I am seventeen now, but back then I was only eleven years old. Zero was the first friend I and both of my brothers had made after moving to Sunnyslope, and we had so many great memories together. Jon and Zero were both thirteen and in eighth grade back then and had become best friends almost instantly. The two of them are nineteen now, and have changed a lot since then. Zero was more slender compared to the three of us, and he also had brown hair but with brown eyes, and he was usually recognized by his purple and black striped zip hoodie that he always had on, no matter what the weather was like. He also always wore a flat brim skateboarding hat with his hood up and tight skate pants that would constantly fall because the shoelace he used as a belt wasn't enough to keep them up.

As the years went by, we all slowly started to mature, although it never showed when we got together because we would do the same stupid stuff we had always done. At that point, Jeff and I raced to go meet up with Jon and Zero every day when we got out of school. From the summer of 2005, right before I started middle school, through the fall of 2009 when I started my freshman year, the four of us spent almost every day together skating and causing trouble everywhere we went.

By the time Jon, Zero, and I got to high school, we had all made a few more friends in the BD classes. The BD Hallway was a secluded hall at Sunnyslope High and was a home away from home for our whole group of friends. The BD hall was where all of our lockers and classrooms were located to keep us all segregated from the rest of the school. BD was an abbreviation for Behavioral Disordered, a term used to describe youths who tended to rebel against society's rules in favor of their own. These teens often acted out because of troubled home lives, learning disabilities, mental health issues, abuse, or trauma.

The BD classes helped me a lot in school, given that all of my friends that were still in high school had classes together. It was rare if I had a class without at least one of my closest friends in it. Our friend group was composed of BD kids of all ages, and the oldest one, Colin, graduated back in 2007. I was put in these classes due to my ditching, not doing my homework, constantly getting in trouble with my friends, and now I can also assume that my mental health issues contributed as well.

It was in the fall of 2009, during his junior year, that Zero got expelled from high school for getting more than ten out-of-school suspensions, and he was sent to a BD school. It was something so small and stupid at the time, but it would go on to ripple out into something awful. A Behavioral Disordered school was a lot worse than the BD hallway. While most of the kids in the BD hallway were trouble makers, they weren't bad people. In the BD school, however, the kids were dangerous. Most of them were gangbangers and drug dealers. The school was basically a juvenile hall. The teachers at the school were trained and legally allowed to use force on a kid who was acting out or was refusing to listen. Zero got into trouble and rebelled often, but I think he knew he didn't belong at that school. I think being away from his friends at a place like that made all of his problems worse. Zero didn't even finish his junior year before deciding to drop out and get his GED.

From what I understand, It was a challenge for Zero when he started the GED process, given he had no money and no car. It took a couple of years, but he finally managed to almost catch up to all of his peers. During those years, he reflected on his life and wondered how everything could fall apart all at once. He noticed the differences between the people who cared about him and wanted what was best for him and the people who only liked him as someone to party with, and he was shown who his real friends were. I also assume he realized the harsh truth that just because something made you happy didn't mean it wasn't bad for you.

We surprisingly had only talked about it once or twice, but Zero also struggled with his own mental health issues. From what I understand, being at that school only made his depression and anxiety worse. Most days he wouldn't even leave the house because all of his friends were at school or working. Zero went from smoking weed in order to help him relax or sleep, to smoking to get high and forget about his problems.

Given he only had a part-time job, Zero couldn't afford the amount of weed he smoked in a day. He became more and more desperate for money, and he eventually switched to pills and then started abusing his anti-anxiety prescriptions. His pill addiction got increasingly worse, to the point where he would finish a whole month's worth of medication in just a few days. Then he would go through terrible withdrawals, experience overwhelming anxiety, and feel depressed for the next three weeks until he could refill his meds and start the process all over again.

Eventually, Zero's addiction got so bad that he reached out to some of the kids he had met at the BD school and asked them if they knew anyone he could buy the pills from. He hadn't seen me, Jon, Jeff, or any of his real friends since he had gotten expelled, and we had slowly drifted apart. So he had been forced to face a lot of his issues alone, and I guess he just felt a lot better not being alone anymore, even if he was starting to hangout with the wrong people. This is when he was introduced to a sketchy man who called himself Chronic.

When Zero first met Chronic, he seemed like a friend. Zero told him all about his situation and everything going on in his life. Chronic was very sympathetic and often told Zero that he could relate to him. This made Zero feel a lot better since he didn't have anyone else to talk to about his problems.

Chronic was also able to get his hands on some of the pills Zero was taking and sell him some for a good price.

"I know how you feel man," he told Zero.

"Sometimes you just need help waking up, getting through your day, and going to sleep at the end of it. Lucky for us, there's different drugs for all of that." Chronic and Zero both laughed.

Zero tried different types of drugs, which helped him with his stress, insomnia, and getting out of bed. As he tried more and more drugs, part of Zero knew he shouldn't be doing this. He was just in too much pain to care, however, and after taking the pills for some time, his tolerance grew. It was at this point that Chronic told Zero,

"Try a line of this. It'll help. Trust me."

"What is it?" Zero asked

"It's just a little bit of Coke," Chronic told him.

"It'll wake you up. You look tired as hell, man."

So, that's what Zero started doing whenever he ran out of pills. What he didn't know at the time was that a lot of drug dealers like Chronic liked to lie about what they were giving people. What he had given Zero wasn't just Coke. It was actually Fentanyl mixed with Oxycodone. He lived in denial for a long time, but, eventually, he had to admit to himself that he wasn't just taking anxiety medication to help with all of his problems anymore. As he became an addict, the drug completely took over his life, and when he got fired from the only job he could find, he hit rock bottom. He created an even bigger problem for himself when he became addicted to heroin.

The first time Zero overdosed, Chronic dragged him out of his car and left him on the side of the road to die. It was then that Zero finally decided to reach out to his real friends. At that point, though, we had already heard that he was doing drugs, and we were angry and upset with him and the road he chose to go down. From our point of view, Zero had just stopped talking to us and started hanging out with new friends, who he did drugs and partied with instead. I felt like he didn't want to hang out with us anymore because we didn't do drugs.

Jon and I had to find out through word of mouth that Zero was an addict, and though we refused to believe it at first, we eventually had to accept that it was true. We were so disappointed with and resentful of him that Jon could hardly talk to him, and I didn't talk to him at all. I responded by not wanting to think about it. We also decided to hide Zero's situation from Jeff as much as we could. He was still so young, and we knew it would break his heart, as it did ours.

"Let's not tell Jeff about Zero," Jon had told me.

"Yeah, I agree, let's act like nothing happened," I had responded.

By the time Zero finally reached out a couple of years later, I was so angry with him and already going through such a hard time myself that I ignored him. Jon did respond, although he couldn't help but be short with him. Zero also sent me messages every other day. "What are you doing?" he would ask. Or he would say, "Let's meet up soon," or "Call me back, bro."

Every message I saw instantly made me sad and angry, and I immediately closed out of every message I read. I had a lot of problems too, but I didn't turn to drugs, I had ignorantly said to myself, filled with resentment. All the while I was reminded of the good times we all had together and how they all came to an end. I wanted to focus on finding things that made me happy. What Jon and I didn't realize at the time, is that we should have put our feelings aside and at least tried to help our friend, but when you're young, you don't think about the possibility of losing a friend. You just figure that none of you will die for a long time, but sadly that's not true.

"It was good to see him," said Jon with a big smile, when, after what felt like hours later, he got back into the car and closed the door behind him. I was jolted back to the present. We sat in silence for a few minutes until eventually he began talking about Sweetheart, which I assume was his attempt at cheering me up. He knew I couldn't help but smile when I thought of her. What I didn't know at the time was that my selfishly staying in the car and refusing to say hi to Zero would be a decision that would haunt me for the rest of my life.

Chapter 2

The Windy City Crusaders

It was a few months later, during the fall of my senior year, that we found out Zero had passed away. On October 2nd, in the middle of the night as everyone else slept, Zero overdosed on heroin and died in his bed. His mother found him in the morning after he hadn't come out of his room.

"Jay…come here quick!" I heard Jon yell, and I jumped and ran towards his room to see what was wrong.

"What?" I said, my heart beating fast. By the tone of his voice and the expression on his face, I knew that something awful must have happened.

"I got a voicemail from Zero's Ma saying that he passed away last night," said Jon, with worry all over his face.

I was speechless as he told me how he woke up to his phone ringing but missed the call from Zero's mom telling him what had happened. Jon went on to explain how he noticed that he had a missed call from Zero last night while he was sleeping. That's when Jon yelled for me and told me everything, but as I looked down at my phone, in shock from what I had just heard, I realized Zero had never tried to call me. I knew I had been ignoring him for a while, but I figured he still would've reached out to me if he thought he was about to die. Or if he planned to die.

Jon and I drove over to Zero's house in denial, hoping it was somehow not true. I sat numbly thinking about how selfish, immature, and stupid I had been. How could I have turned my back on someone who was like an older brother to me? I realized that he was probably asking me for help. I had figured we would eventually work things out, but I had known Zero was hanging out with the wrong people, and I couldn't even handle my own problems, never mind his. At the time, I didn't know that it helps you when you help others. I had been ignorant of what the real world is actually like.

When we pulled up to Zero's house, I couldn't even get out of the car. I was too ashamed of myself. I became extremely anxious, and I didn't want to look into Zero's mother's eyes, knowing that I hadn't been there for her son when he had needed his friends. From the car, I watched Jon walk right up the driveway and hug Zero's mom and brother, comforting them as he fought back tears of his own. After a little time had passed, Jon returned to the car to see how I was doing, and he confirmed my worst fear. I was just standing by the car, looking at the ground thinking, and trying not to cry.

Jon looked at me.

"Are you okay?"

"We have to go find Jeff. We should be there when he finds out," I responded, ignoring Jon's question and trying to keep myself from crying any more.

Jon put his head down, looking like he was, again, trying not to cry himself. I imagined that the fact that he had lost his childhood best friend was starting to sink in. I thought about how hard it was gonna hit Jeff and dreaded having to tell him. Jeff looked up to Zero even more than I did. How are we gonna break the news to him? I asked myself. Jon must have been thinking something similar.

"Let's go find him," he said to me as he got into the car.

Jeff was at the skate park when we told him what happened. Little Jeff put his face into his hands and started crying immediately. Jon and I both hugged him, and then each of us put an arm around him and walked him to the car to take him home. Zero was Jeff's idol, and Jeff had always copied everything he did. I hated myself when I looked at Jeff's purple and black hoodie. He had gotten the same one as Zero, and seeing it reminded me of how I had let Zero down.

"How did he die?" Jeff asked, his eyes filled with tears.

Me and Jon looked at each other with tears in our eyes as well before Jon lied,

"His heart gave out." I wanted to tell Jeff the truth eventually, so he would know not to start taking drugs

23

also. For now, though, I didn't have it in me to argue with Jon or cause any of us any more pain.

Other than the sounds of crying, the car was completely silent. I again looked down at my phone, and, once again, thought about how Zero never tried to call me, and I felt even more horrible. The regret I felt at the thought of Zero going to the grave alone at such a young age, thinking no one cared about him, was something I could not forgive myself for. Even if I couldn't have done anything about it, I could've at least been there, so he knew we all cared.

Why didn't I get out of the car to talk to him?

Every time you walk up to an open casket and see someone you care about inside, it's always a mix of emotions. The body never seems to look like the person you knew. You know it's them, but at the same time, it doesn't feel like it's actually them. They look more like a waxed statue created by an awful artist. At least that's how I felt while at the wake, looking at one of my oldest friends in his coffin.

The day of Zero's funeral was one of the hardest days of my life. It was bad enough losing him and feeling responsible for his death, but on top of that, the anxiety I felt being around all of those people at the service made it so much worse. Zero's death also hit our family hard, as they cared deeply for him too. It wasn't just Jon, Jeff, and I who cared about Zero. He had become an adoptive member of our family, given how often he came over throughout our childhood. Now he was gone.

I watched, struggling to control my emotions, and could tell Jon and Jeff did as well, as Zero's coffin sat inside the hole in the ground. We all knew we would never see our brother again. I thought about all the things he would never get to do and about all the memories we all could have made together in the future.

Later, while Jon comforted Jeff and a few other friends who were close to Zero, I stayed isolated. Reliving the old memories brought smiles to my brothers' faces, but it only reminded me of my mistakes. I kept to myself the fact that Zero never called me. I also later found out that Zero had called a few of my friends and not just Jon. Though I didn't know for sure if Zero purposely didn't call me or if he had just died before he had the chance to, I saw it as if Zero didn't even bother, as if he knew he couldn't count on me.

My insomnia became worse after Zero's death. I went on walks for hours when I couldn't sleep. I thought about everything that had happened, but no matter how far or where I walked, I always ended up in the same place. At St. Matthew Cemetery. I always hopped the fence and entered the graveyard to stand by Zero's grave for long periods of time. I would apologize to Zero and talk about all the things I should have done differently.

"I'm sorry," I said countless times.

"I promise not to turn my back on a friend ever again," I thought about an alternate universe, one where I had responded to him, one where we met up with him and helped him, one where he got sober and got to live the rest of his life, but I knew it was too late now.

One night, I stood at the graveyard taking in the fall breeze, thinking about all the kids who were now addicted to drugs, about how everybody thought selling drugs was cool, and how half of the dealers wouldn't get into trouble even if they were caught because their parents were rich. I shook my head thinking about the fact that everyone on both sides of town hated the BD kids.

The Southside and most of the upper class and upper middle class citizens were very stuck up and judged anyone who wasn't one of them, while at the same time they constantly looked down on others, as if their own beliefs made them good people even though they were just as bad as everybody else. The only difference was that they got away with everything because of their money and connections. Even most of the cops in Sunnyslope thought the same way they did, pretending that the root of any issue within Sunnyslope was the lower-class Northsiders.

The Northside was just as bad but for different reasons. Because we were a low income family, my family and I were considered Northsiders, but we didn't fit in with them either. Most of the lower class also thought that their opposing beliefs made them good people as well, despite idolizing gangbangers and drug dealers. This always aggravated me. My grandfather had been a gangster when he was younger and spent the second half of his life trying to atone for all that he had done. He taught me and my brothers just how evil the people like that truly were and to stay away from that life.

The Northside blamed the rich for everything and also took no responsibility for anything.I couldn't stand either side. I didn't understand how people could defend or make excuses for either of them. The only difference between them was who they empathized with. The ones who didn't do drugs accused us of selling drugs, while the ones that did gave us grief for not taking any drugs. Most of us had substance abusers in our family and knew not to go down that road.

I thought about my Ma, who'd been saying for years that she wanted to leave Sunnyslope because of how awful both sides were. I also thought about my peers who constantly drove past us yelling insults from the safety of their parents' cars to remind us how we didn't fit in with either side or feel like we belonged anywhere. I thought about how the cops, the school, and the mayor refused to do anything about the drug problem. They lived in denial and wanted to keep the issue quiet in order to protect the town's reputation.

These thoughts continued to intrude my mind, spreading like a forest fire until all of the sudden a crack of lightning lit up the sky, and a gust of wind pushed my hair aside as a bunch of leaves flew around everywhere. Tears fell from my eyes. My sadness, guilt, and dislike for confrontation and violence quickly turned to anger, rage, and an urge to atone. Someone needed to do something. That's when I came up with a plan.

Seven days before Halloween, I sat in the booth at Misfits, the local diner. I had asked my three best friends, Chish, D, and Ski Ski, to meet me to discuss my plan. I decided to talk to the three of them before telling my brothers or the rest of my friends my idea. I normally confided in them first because if these three weren't convinced it was a good idea, and if I couldn't get them to agree to help, then there was no point in asking the others.

Ski Ski was the first to show up. Ski Ski was the first friend I made back when my family moved to Sunnyslope six years earlier. We met in our first period English class, shortly after my brothers and I had met Zero, and the two of us always joked around and got into trouble for distracting all the other kids in the class.

Ski Ski was a very pale and slender kid of average height, with long black greasy hair. He was the type of friend who made me constantly ask myself why I hung out with him. He was disloyal, narcissistic, stole from his friends, and started fights all the time. He constantly lied to everyone about everything and spoke ill about everybody behind their backs. Yet, the truth was that Jon, Jeff, and I had so many fun memories with him that we couldn't bring ourselves to drop him as a friend.

I'm done talking to him, I said to myself I don't know how many times. Having a friend like Ski Ski could give you a lot of trust issues and become unforgiving to the people who didn't deserve it. It took me a while to realize all of this, but after the pain of losing Zero and the promise I made to him that I wouldn't turn my back on a friend again, it made me wanna help Ski Ski even more. So, now I was more unwilling than ever to walk away from Ski Ski. I didn't want to risk losing another friend.

"So what's up?" said Chish as he sat down in the booth a few minutes after Ski Ski showed up. I was in seventh grade when I met Chris, a.k.a Chish, and D. Chish had brown hair and blue eyes, and he was always a shy kid, due to moving a lot with his mom and siblings from Poland and then back and forth to different towns throughout the Chicagoland area. This is why he also struggled with social skills. He and I easily connected since we both liked skateboarding and both of us had a hard time talking to people, ironic considering we had met in social studies class.

Chish's social issues weren't nearly as bad as mine, but he was socially awkward enough to have an idea of what I struggled with. Since we both had social issues, we could understand and give advice to each other about making friends, speaking in front of the class, and talking to girls. Advice that we really couldn't find anywhere else. Chish and I became close when we just so happened to be seated right next to each other in class, and the two of us, who were normally quiet, eventually became comfortable enough around each other to the point that our teacher had to constantly tell us to stop talking. What was also ironic is that both my older brother Jon and his Greg, both two grades older than us, went on to become friends as well. When Jon, Greg, and Zero would ditch school every day together.

"Yeah, why did you ask all of us to meet you here?" said D, after shaking everyone's hand. He looked around, and I assumed this was to see if he recognized anyone else at the restaurant. Then he looked towards Ski Ski, who was on his phone. D not only showed up last but late as well. Which didn't surprise me. I laugh every time I think about when D and I first met. It was in seventh grade in guided study hall, a.k.a BD study hall, and the two of us had become friends immediately.

D had black hair and brown eyes and was drastically different from Chish and me. He was always a big guy compared to his peers. He wore a size sixteen shoe in seventh grade and somehow managed to become a decent skateboarder, despite his shoe almost being as big as the board itself. D was always loyal and there for his friends whenever we needed him. D was the friend who could make you laugh on the worst day of your life.

I would go to Chish to talk about a problem, but I would go to D when I needed to have fun and get my mind off of my problems. On the other hand, I usually hid my problems from Ski Ski. He only made them worse or told other people everything I had said to him in confidence. D and I brought out the no filter, trouble maker side of each other. We would insult and take turns exchanging witty remarks to each other in the middle of class and then get sent to our dean all the time, and when we would get an out-of-school suspension for swearing or fighting with each other, we would just meet up and go to the skate park as if nothing happened.

It got to the point where our dean would only give us in-school suspensions because we openly admitted that we liked getting out-of-school suspensions. All that we would have to do was make sure not to get more than ten of them so we wouldn't get expelled. So towards the end of the school year, we would just bite our tongue and suddenly become the best-behaved kids in the BD hallway until the school year ended, and when the next year began, we would start the process all over again. This, of course, infuriated some of our teachers and our dean. Ski Ski, D, Chish, and I had every class together since we were all the same age and had all of our classes in the BD hall, and the poor teachers never stood a chance. When we got to high school, our ditching, swearing, and back and forth insults only got worse.

I took a deep breath, and looked around the diner to make sure no one else could hear us. I was getting anxious, since I knew that things didn't always go as I planned. I was really good at predicting different possible outcomes in almost any given situation, though I also spent so much time inside my own head that I sometimes completely misjudged how a person would react or how a situation would play out. I had a tendency to idealize people, places, and situations, while at the same time, I could make things out to be worse than they actually were.

"Look, you guys know what happened to Zero. D and Ski Ski, you guys used to be close friends with him also, and, Chish, your older brother is dealing with the same issues that killed Zero. It's the drug dealers in our town from the North and Southside who are getting kids hooked on heroin because they think selling drugs makes them rebellious. We need to stop them. My plan is to get you three, Andy, Colin, Sarge, Anthony, Jon, and Jeff all together. Then the ten of us go find all the dealers in Sunnyslope and stop all of them, take the drugs from them, and find out where they are getting all of it from. All that we would have to do is to make them afraid to sell any drugs again. Then no one else will become addicted, and no one else has to die of an overdose because they won't be able to find any drugs."

The other three paused and looked at each other, then back at me for what felt like an unusually long time. I immediately started to worry that this was another situation where I had spent so much time thinking about how everyone would think I had such a great idea that I never stopped to consider the possibility that some of my friends may not agree with me.

"Look," D said,

"I know The Dark Knight is your favorite movie. And you've rewatched DBZ like thirteen times because it's your favorite TV show, and you're obsessed with superheroes, but that idea seems a little crazy to me."

I couldn't help but get a little angry and defensive with him. It felt like he wasn't just disagreeing with me, but he was also insulting me. I decided to play it off as humor, though.

"If you don't like The Dark Knight and DBZ, then we were never friends," I said as they all laughed.

"I've always hated you," said D, adding to the laughter.

"So what, we just fight them, and that will make them stop selling drugs?" Chish asked.

"To be honest, I don't think that'll get them to stop," he added after laughing and taking a few moments to think about it.

I started to feel angry again. Chish and D were the ones I expected to agree right away. It was Ski Ski who I imagined would have needed convincing.

"If we hurt them badly enough, it will, and if we find out how they are getting the drugs, we'll stop them for sure," I replied, aggravated.

"Well, I'm down," Ski Ski said, as I looked at him. I was surprised, given the fact that Ski Ski normally praised gangsters and drug dealers.

How many times had he begged me to tell him more stories about Grandpa's past? Now he had a problem with it? Maybe Zero's death changed his mind, I thought to myself. I smiled and nodded at Ski Ski, seeing a glimpse of hope for him.

"Okay, fine. Me too. Let's find them and give it a try for Zero," D added.

"I mean, I guess we could. If you think that'll help?" said Chish, not sounding very optimistic.

Always the realistic one about everything. I, on the other hand, felt a surge of excitement knowing he was starting to come around also.

"Chish you're always so pessimistic man," said D, shaking his head

"Alright yeah, fine, let's do it," Chish agreed.

"Maybe we could stop them. I don't want my brother to lose his life over this stuff. When and how will we know who's selling drugs?" he added, raising his eyebrows and forcing a smile before taking a drink of his water.

I smiled, feeling happy and hopeful.

"I'm gonna ask Colin to ask around and see who's selling and where, since he knows everyone. Once we get this information we can hunt them all down and attack. We can do it on Halloween, since that's the next time everyone's gonna be out partying and looking to get high, which means a lot of dealers will be selling all around town."

"Alright, cool. Let us know when you find out more," said Chish

"This is gonna be awesome," said Ski Ski

"Yeah, I'll ask around too," said D.

I felt a rush of excitement come over me. They were actually agreeing to this.

"Okay, but try to keep it quiet, though. We don't want anyone, especially the dealers, to find out about our plan. I'll talk to everyone else to get them to agree to help and let you guys know more about how we're gonna do this." I felt more confident about my plan now that all three of them agreed to help. I was right to talk to them first.

We're gonna find and stop all of them for you, Zero, I said to myself as I left the restaurant after saying goodbye to my friends. Now that I had the three of them on board to help, I needed to individually talk to Andy, Colin, Sarge, and Anthony.

First, I went to see my friend Andy. He wasn't at work so I knew that he must have been at the gym. Andy was a lifelong friend of my family and basically grew up with us. He met Jon way back in first grade and was now nineteen years old. Andy was a very quiet, honorable, and respectful Irish and Navajo kid, covered in tattoos. He was very loyal to my family, especially Jon. Wherever Jon was, you could always find Andy close by, and no matter what the situation, Andy would always have Jon's back and look out for his little brothers and family. Even after my family moved away from the old neighborhood, we kept in touch with Andy, and we would visit each other as often as possible. After Andy graduated high school, he decided to move to

35

Sunnyslope to reunite and stay with us. That's when he started working at The Chirish Pub with Colin.

"What do you think?" I said to Andy after explaining my idea to him.

"Okay, if that's what you guys wanna do, man," replied Andy with a heartfelt expression.

"I'll always have your back." he finished before he continued to hit the heavy bag.

Next, I went to visit Colin at the bar and discussed the plan over a couple of rounds of pool. Colin was twenty-two and the oldest member of the Group. He was a senior in high school back in 2006 when he first met Jon, who had just entered his freshmen year. Not long after, he became close friends with Jon and, therefore, me and Jeff as well. Despite being in the BD classes, Colin was very social and somehow knew everyone, and everybody loved him. He was always making jokes and telling stories and could easily make friends anywhere he went. I honestly envied his social skills and thought it was impressive, as well as a little annoying, how he couldn't go anywhere in the Chicagoland area without bumping into someone he knew, and every time he ran into a friend or an acquaintance, he would, of course, have to have a long conversation and reminisce about memories they'd shared.

After he finished high school, Colin started working at The Chirish Pub, where everyone would stop by to see him. He went on to become a bouncer and then bartender, and even though most of the Group was too young to sit at the bar, we would play pool and get food while he was working, just so we could visit him. At least until midnight came around, which was when they kicked out anyone who wasn't twenty-one or older. Colin was also Irish, had a big beard, and constantly wore a backward hat. He wasn't always the most reliable friend, partly having to do with the fact that he considered so many people to be his friend, but he had always been there for the three of us when we needed him.

"Fine, if doing this will stop everybody from dying, then, hell yeah, I'm down," said Colin, nodding up and down as he smacked one of the pool balls into a pocket at the pub.

Next up was Sarge. I stopped by the skatepark to pay him a visit. Sarge was nineteen and was a friend that we got close with back when I was a sophomore in high school. He lived just a few blocks away from my family, and he and Jon met by sharing the same bus throughout their freshmen and sophomore years. Sarge was always a friendly and very respectful guy, despite how mean and scary he looked. I could relate to him, given that he, too, was often misjudged by everybody until they got a chance to meet him. I assume he was misjudged mainly due to his very tall liberty-spiked mohawk and his spiked leather jacket. He also always wore combat boots with ripped jeans and a sleeveless shirt, even in the winter. He was of average height and had brown hair, but it was hard to tell since it was usually covered in glue to keep the mohawk up. Sarge was a really good friend, and he was at one point one of both mine and Jon's best friends.

"You know what dude, let's give it a try. I've been thinking the same thing, man. Someone's gotta stop these scumbags. I'm in." Sarge sounded both angry and excited as we sat at the skatepark watching the skaters skate.

Finally, there was Anthony. Despite being a humble and laid-back person, he also had a temper, and if you managed to get under his skin, you'd regret it. Anthony was about to be twenty-one. He had curly hair and was half black and half Italian. I met Anthony at his place. Similar to me and my brothers, he was also raised by his mom and grandma. Colin had introduced Jon, Jeff, and me to a lot of people, and Anthony would swiftly go on to become one of our closest and most trusted friends. Due to our identical backgrounds, a mutual love of skateboarding, and our similar tastes in music and TV shows.

Anthony was one of those people you met and knew right away that you'd be friends for life. He was always very talented when it came to music. He could play multiple instruments, sing, and could even cross different genres of music easily. Everyone who knew Anthony knew that he would go on to become successful with music one way or another. Anthony was the friend that Jon and sometimes I would go to when we needed advice on something. He always told you his honest opinion, even if it wasn't what you wanted to hear, and he always had good advice for whatever situation you were in. Anthony was sometimes quiet and inside his head thinking about new music, while at other times he was extremely social and the life of the party.

When I got to Anthony's house, he was sitting on his bed with his guitar. After I told him the plan, he took his hands off his guitar and threw them in the air.

"Um...yeah, why not? I'm always down to back up my friends," he said emotionlessly. I couldn't help but laugh at how casual he was about it. Even though some of my friends weren't that close to Zero themselves, still they decided to help anyway because they all knew how much me, Jon, and Jeff cared about Zero, not to mention so many kids we all grew up with or met had died at this point, I knew that they had lost some friends also.

So, Colin agreed to ask around and find out some info, and in the meantime, I had to talk to Jon and Jeff. I had decided to ask Jon and Jeff last. I wasn't sure if Jeff was old enough, given he was only in eighth grade, and I already knew that when I did ask Jeff, he would say yes right away anyways. It was Jon I dreaded talking to about it because he always challenged everything I thought or said, and I also knew that Jon hated fighting outside of the gym. So I knew the hardest one to convince would be him.

I really struggled with whether or not I wanted Jeff to come with us. I wanted to let Jeff just be a kid while he could and stay oblivious to how awful the world could be. My mind started to mess with me, and I feared that what happened to Zero could happen to my little brother too. The obsessive thoughts of Jeff or anyone else I cared about in a coffin also becoming an addict or dying terrified me so much and made me so angry, I couldn't think straight. So, I wanted Jeff to at the very least come along with us to see he could see for himself and understand what was happening. I figured I would just tell Jeff that he wasn't allowed to fight and to just keep an eye out for cops, and I would ask everyone to keep an eye on him. Just as I predicted, Jeff agreed instantly, but he was mad when I told him he couldn't fight.

"Why not?" he asked.

"Now that you have told me the truth about what happened with Zero, I wanna help stop them." Jeff pleaded with me, eager to get revenge for what had happened to Zero, but I told him,

"No, Jeff, you're too young to fight them. The dealers are in high school or older. The rest of us can't focus on them if we have to worry about you getting hurt."

Meanwhile, also as expected, Jon disagreed with my plan, and we got into an argument over it, although he did agree that something needed to be done.

"Going around town attacking drug dealers isn't going to solve this, Jay. I like that you got everybody together, and I'm ready to help, but there's another way," Jon said in his usual stubborn manner, treating me like he always knew more than I did.

"How then?" I asked, immediately aggravated since I knew Jon would respond this way and was starting to get sick of everyone immediately criticizing my plan without offering up any other ideas or solutions.

"I don't know yet, but we can figure it out," said Jon. I could tell he was starting to get angry, himself, and Jeff got noticeably worried. He got in between us in case he had to stop us if a punch was thrown.

"Okay, well let me know when you do. Until then, this is what the rest of us are doing," I said, walking away just to end the conversation and avoid a fight.

Jon had always loved boxing, and he was trained by our grandfather, who was an amateur boxer back during World War 2 while he was a paratrooper in the army. Out of all three of us, Jon liked fighting the most. He would usually view his opponent as a sparring partner rather than an enemy. He saw fighting as a way to improve his skills, and he would rise to whatever challenge presented itself.

Yet, while Jon always enjoyed fighting, he never went looking for fights, and he hated fighting outside of the gym. The only time he would be serious in a fight was when he fought to defend someone else. Jon had gotten into two different fist fights with middle-aged men before he had even turned eighteen, and he won both of them with ease. No matter who Jon fought, he always found a way to win, but even if he lost, he would just learn from his mistakes and improve upon his skills. I always admired that about Jon, and even when we fought with each other, I still respected him.

Later that day, after Jon, still angry from the argument by the look on his face, told me that he decided that he'd go with us to look out for his brothers and his friends, while at the same time try to prevent us from hurting anyone too badly. I guessed he could tell that if I, who he would normally have to beg to fight him for fun in the ring, was now seeking out conflict, it must have been obvious that I was really serious about doing this for Zero. Jon probably realized that the only thing he could do for now, though, was to just try and think of another plan before something really bad happened, and what I didn't know at the time was that most of the Group actually agreed with Jon. They just decided to keep it too themselves and see if my plan actually helped, since they had no other solutions.

It felt like it had been two years instead of two weeks since Zero had passed on October 2nd, and as Halloween approached, I planned out exactly what we would do. After Colin asked around and gathered all the information we needed, I told everyone the plan for the night. We decided to split everybody into two groups to cover more ground and hopefully find more dealers throughout the town. My group included me, Chish, D,

Sarge, and Ski Ski, and our mission was to search for the Northside dealers. Meanwhile, Jon, Jeff, Colin, Anthony, and Andy would find the Southside dealers.

Jon told me,

"I'll only go along with your plan if you look out for everyone in your group, you guys promise not to hurt anyone too badly, and if Jeff goes with my group."

"Fine, as long as Jeff is aware of what is happening. And I'll look out for my group, and you look out for yours," I said as me, Jon, and Jeff all nodded at each other. Each group would take a couple of local spots where Colin had heard where dealers might be selling.

Me, Chish, D, Sarge, and Ski Ski went after the Northside dealers. We started by Highway Hill, a street running under the highway that connected Sunnyslope to another town and took you to and from the city. Highway Hill was also right next to the Prarie Path, a bike trail that ran throughout three different counties and various towns in Illinois. The trail was normally used by bikers or runners for exercise, but at night the surrounding darkness and trees gave dealers a secluded place to sell drugs.

I was anxious at first, approaching the dealers while knowing there was about to be a fight. They were all talking and smiling with one another as we skated towards them, and we tried to confront them as quickly as possible. Ski Ski almost fell off his board, his eyes were so focused on the dealers. None of the dealers knew what was gonna happen yet. There is always a big risk of something terrible happening whenever you get into even the smallest conflict, and I tried to keep that in the back of my mind the whole night.

There were a few guys dealing and a couple of buyers standing outside their cars picking up drugs from the dealers. They must have assumed for a second that we were looking to buy some, but to their shock, we attacked and quickly started fighting. Ski Ski, always willing to start a fight as long as he had back up to save him, threw the first punch, but he immediately started losing,

"What's your problem man?" asked one of the dealers. He hit Ski Ski back and knocked him to the ground. Chish, Sarge, and D jumped in to rescue the damsel in distress and started throwing punches at the other three dealers to defend Ski Ski.

Meanwhile, I quickly snatched the drugs out of the buyer's hands before jumping in myself. It wasn't hard, since I could tell they were both confused and frozen in fear.

"Leave and don't let us find you buying anything from them again!" I said, realizing that I wasn't as socially anxious as usual. I felt even more confident once I noticed this.

"Let's get out of here," one of the buyers said and ran off, leaving their car behind.

I immediately punched the dealer who was manhandling Ski Ski and started fighting alongside my friends. The fight didn't last much longer, though. At that point, the dealers lay on the ground in pain and looked up in shock and terror at the five of us.

"Tell us where you guys got the drugs now!" said Sarge

"No, go to hell," said one of the dealers before getting kicked in the face as D planted his large shoe back onto the ground.

"You better watch who you're talking to and answer the question," said Sarge

"Okay, Okay! A guy who calls himself Chronic gave it to us to sell. We're just trying to make some money, man," replied the dealer immediately, a mixture of pain and fear in his voice. D and I looked at each other.

That's the guy we heard Zero use to bought from.

"Even if you need money, that doesn't justify killing people," said Chish

"We're not killing anybody," said another dealer, scowling angrily.

"They chose to buy from us. They are killing themselves."

"Not anymore! You're probably the same type of scumbags who complain about crooked cops and corrupt politicians but then praise gangsters and drug lords, like there's a difference. I guarantee none of you have even met a real gangster. If you had and still think that they are cool, then you're either brainless, heartless, or both," I said, feeling more assertive. I could tell that everyone on both sides stopped to think about what they had just heard.

"Now tell us where we can find him!" I added. The dealers avoided eye contact while they appeared to still be thinking about what I said.

"We don't know," said another one, who I recognized from school.

"He doesn't live in Sunnyslope. He's from the city."

"Now you know who we are, and we know who you are. Next time you sell drugs in our town, we'll be back for you," said Sarge. I started to walk away, and I nodded to my friends to come with me. We all left with a surge of excitement and adrenaline, looking forward to finding more dealers.

My group then made it Uptown and caught some more dealers in the underpass, which was located underneath the Sunnyslope train station. Me and Sarge, then D, Ski Ski, and Chish all split up and cut them off on both sides as we began fighting again. This time there was no one picking up from them, so we didn't have to worry about mistaking an addict for a dealer. We didn't hold back at all.

"You guys are monsters, man. What did we do to you?" asked one of the dealers, cowering in fear.

"I'm not a monster. You're the monster," I said to him softly, feeling my eyes dry out from not blinking. I was breathing heavily.

The fight was similar to our encounter with the first dealers, though slightly more brutal, and we got no information on Chronic after interrogating them as well. It seemed that the dealers knew as little about Chronic as we did. The scumbag was smart. He must have known not to give too many personal details to anyone. He probably expected the cops would eventually find him if he did, I thought to myself as we skated away, still angry about being called a monster.

The last stop of the night and the place where we would all meet was at the skatepark. As all of us approached the park together, there were, fortunately, no dealers to be found, and given that the cops were now out and about, it was a relief. Both groups got together at the skatepark, and I collected all of the drugs we had gathered from the multiple dealers, unsure of what to do with all of them. I decided that I would figure that out later. For now, I just didn't want to get caught by the cops with any of it.

"We should call it a night before the cops catch up with us," Jon said to everyone.

"Yeah, I agree," I said, even though I wanted to keep going.

"What happened with you guys?" I asked Anthony who filled me in on how the night went for them. He said that when he, Jon, Jeff, Colin, and Andy hit the Southside dealers they went straight to Sunnyslope High. They headed towards the school, knowing that some people hung out at the football field when there wasn't a football game. As they walked around the field, it didn't take long for them to discover a few dealers, though the dealers were also quick to spot the group approaching. As soon as Jon's group, starting with Jeff, had charged them, they took off running, but Anthony came flying through the field in his car and reached out of his window and grabbed one of them. Anthony's doing that caused enough of a distraction to give the rest of them time to grab the other dealers. The second group finished the fight just as quickly as the first.

"You are destroying families and ruining people's lives, and it stops now, please!" Jon pleaded with the injured dealers.

"And we don't care who your parents are or how much money your family has. You guys are done," said Colin.

Meanwhile, Jeff walked toward the group and said,

"That's it? We are gonna just let them go? We have to hurt them more than that to make them stop."

"No Jeff! We're leaving. They've had enough. Go get in the car," said Jon as Jeff angrily walked away as the other four followed behind towards Anthony's car to head to the next spot.

After they finished up at the school, they went to the parking garage behind the local movie theater, which was also Uptown. The parking garage made catching the dealers a bit of a challenge. The four dealers split up and ran in different directions. Unfortunately for them, though, Jon's group had their skateboards and a car, so splitting up only bought them a little more time. Before the dealers could leave the parking garage, they caught up with them and, after a fight, took their supplies. As Jon's group fought the dealers, though, they also heard the sirens approaching and saw red and blue lights in the distance. They wondered how the cops found out what we were doing. Anthony had assumed the same thing I did. It was most likely a random pedestrian that saw people fighting and decided to call the police, but it didn't matter. It just meant it was time for all of us to leave and head to our final spot before the cops caught up with them.

I felt even more satisfied as I listened to how the other group's night went. The rest of the BD kids shared their stories of how the night went for them as well. I could tell by the expression on his face that Jon looked back on the night with regret, knowing there would be consequences. I felt slightly redeemed after tonight, but I knew that wasn't enough to make up for what I had done to Zero, and it definitely wasn't enough to solve the drug problem in Sunnyslope. After all, we didn't get any information on Chronic. Still, it felt like it was a great start. The whole night felt like a superhero movie, and I was ready to keep going.

Chapter 3

Invade.Demolish.Restore

The following day at school, most of my peers had heard what had happened. As I walked through the halls, I overheard multiple conversations and smiled at one point when I heard one of my classmates say,

"Yeah man, that's crazy. I'm not going anywhere near that stuff."

After I got out of my first period class, I ran into Sweetheart. She was not only my only female friend, but she was also the only friend I had at Sunnyslope High who had never been in any BD classes. Fortunately for me, though, she was very talkative and social, so she had been the one to talk to me first. Since conversations, especially ones with a girl as pretty as Sweetheart, were such a challenge to me, I had become smitten instantly after my first encounter with her.

Normally it takes a while for me to let people get close to me, but she was persistent. She dropped kicked right through that barrier I've had up most of my life. I think it was a combination of her childlike personality, her good heart, and her amazing sense of humor. I liked how classy and feisty she was. She was like a mixture of an old lady and a little kid. She always wore sundresses or oversized sweaters and red lipstick. She baked cookies for everybody and bought Christmas presents for the mailman. One day, shortly after meeting, I caught her chasing a bunch of birds and nearly let it slip that I loved her. I'd been cautious since then because I thought I almost ruined our friendship. I could never tell if she felt the same way, since she was so naturally friendly, flirty, outgoing, and always gave everyone she met a big hug. I at least liked to think she also felt that we had a unique bond, given that I was a fusion of an old man and a child myself. We both had young hearts and old souls.

At first I think she noticed how quiet I was and how most of the time I kept to myself, and I must have come off as mysterious since that alone made her curious enough to want to get to know me. Unlike most of my friends, I became comfortable around her immediately. I began to open up more with her and formed a type of connection with her that I've never been able to do with anyone else. She wanted to be friends with me and wouldn't take no for an answer, and I had never been more grateful for such an intrusion.

The rest of my friends and family loved Sweetheart, but, for a long time, Sweetheart's family and friends didn't feel the same about me. There were different reasons as to why I think they didn't like me. Maybe they didn't like that I was a BD kid or that I came from a low-income family and didn't live on the Southside of town or that I was a skater who got into trouble with my friends a lot. Regardless, it never stopped her from hanging out with me because, thankfully, she saw past all those things and gave me a chance.

Today, when I saw Sweetheart, I couldn't help but become excited and smile, but that smile and feeling quickly faded when I noticed how mad she looked. She must have also heard what happened and had come to confront me about it.

"Was that you and your friends that attacked those kids on Halloween?" she asked, clearly already knowing the answer to her question.

"Um... Yeah," I said nervously. I never could lie to her. I tried not to express how terrified I was. I knew she was gonna be furious at me, not only because of what we did on Halloween, but also because I had been avoiding her since Zero died. I knew she would've wanted to be there for me, but I was so angry and full of hate between dealing with my issues and with everything that happened with Zero. I didn't want her to see me like that, and I didn't think that I deserved any comfort. I knew she would try to convince me that it wasn't my fault, and I didn't want to hear it. There was no excuse for what I did. Part of me also was afraid that if she saw me like this, she might start to see me the same way her parents and friends did.

"They were selling drugs, and no one was doing anything about it. Now everyone knows that if you sell drugs, you're gonna get hurt, problem solved," I said like it was no big deal, although I was not even convinced, myself.

"Except for the fact that everybody thinks you guys are a gang and attacked them for no reason," said an annoyed Sweetheart.

"Seriously? The people in this town are so stupid," I responded in disbelief, covering my face with my hand.

"They're not the only ones," said Sweetheart wittingly.

"I'm stupid for wanting to stop anyone else from overdosing or spending the rest of their life battling an addiction?" I was starting to feel irritated towards her, like she was implying that I was no different than the dealers.

"No, you're wrong for thinking that attacking them will solve the problem. This isn't like you. You normally don't like violence." Sweetheart looked more empathetic than angry now. I hated seeing her so upset.

"I don't like violence, but my demons do..." I was feeling angrier by the second.

"Let's find another way to help," said Sweetheart, as she grabbed my hand and pleaded with me. She knew me so well at this point. She was able to figure out what I was feeling about Zero just by gathering some information from my friends and family.

"If you think of one, let me know. Until then I'm not just gonna sit back and watch people die like I did with Zero." I gently pulled my hand away and walked off before I said something to her that I would regret. Those sad eyes were stuck in my head as I left, and I hated myself for upsetting her. She was right. I always loathed violence, but I couldn't help it. The dealers needed to be held responsible for all the lives they've destroyed.

In November, as fall ended and winter began, the Group continued patrolling the streets of Sunnyslope as often as possible, looking for and occasionally fighting different drug dealers, even though Jon and now Sweetheart openly continued to disagree with my approach.

Meanwhile, the rest of the Group tried to show support for both of us because they thought we both had a point. So, Jon focused more on finding another way to solve the problem. He cared more about finding Chronic than finding any of the dealers. After all, I think he understood why I was doing what I was doing. He, too, felt responsible for Zero's death, despite the fact that he had been more responsive than I had towards Zero before he died.

Jeff continued to protest to both me and Jon, demanding that the dealers needed to be punished even more.

"Are you guys stupid? Neither of you is handling it right," he said. Jon thought it would be more effective to focus on helping recovering addicts and educating kids on what was happening than going after the dealers. While from my point of view, it was most effective to start with the root of the problem, Jon thought that knowing what drugs could do to them would stop people from trying any in the first place.

"I can tell them what happened to Zero," he said,

"Explain that I lost my best friend, and they will see that you're never too young to die."

Though Jon had a great point, I quickly countered by telling him that there were already organizations that did that, and kids were still trying drugs. Jon thought that maybe it would be better coming from someone a little closer to them in age, that maybe we would get the message across a lot better.

Jon, Andy, Colin, Anthony, and Sweetheart decided to get a few more kids from the high school and give this new approach a try. They started by talking to the principal of Sunnyslope High. They managed to set up a meeting with her to discuss the problem, but she quickly denied their request to speak to the students and bring attention to the problem.

"She didn't seem surprised by the drug problem at all, and when we told her our idea she told us that it's out of her control and that we would need to talk to the mayor and get his approval first," Sweetheart said, upset.

"I could tell that she just wanted to get rid of us. She didn't want to deal with us or the problem. I imagine it would make her look bad if parents found out students at her school are either selling drugs or becoming heroin addicts. So, we are setting up an appointment with the mayor to hopefully get his help."

Again, my friends waited for a meeting, this time to talk to the mayor, while at the same time, we all continued to search the town for any dealers we could find. Sweetheart told me that to both her and Jon's surprise, the meeting with the mayor was finally scheduled for Thanksgiving. They said they weren't going to think too much into the odd meeting time and stay focused on the meeting itself.

On Wednesday, November 23rd, the day before Thanksgiving, our favorite Sunnyslope police officer stopped by our place for a visit. He was an old friend of Jon, Jeff, and I. He used to be the school cop at Sunnyslope High until he got promoted to detective, and I had nicknamed him Gordon shortly after meeting him. He reminded me of Commissioner James Gordon, the police officer who worked alongside Batman. Similar to the comic book Gordon, our Gordon also had a mustache, dark hair, and a calm demeanor. He was the only cop in town we knew of that didn't bully anyone or abuse his power. He understood the difference between the kids who got into trouble but still had morals and the kids whose parents or circumstances had sadly failed them.

Jon opened the door, and he, Jeff, and I all greeted Gordon.

"Hey Gordon!" we all said at the same time as Gordon shook all of our hands from oldest to youngest.

"Well, I just wanted to stop by and give you guys a heads up. First of all, we all know what happened on Halloween, and I know it was you guys who did it. Fortunately, I'm the only one who knows, or you would be arrested already. The other cops were told that a group of skateboarders attacked a bunch of North and Southside kids, but they left out the part where those kids were selling drugs," said Gordon

"How did you know it was us?" Jeff asked, surprised.

"Because you three brothers and your friends are the only people in this town I know that break the law but also ironically care about what's right. That's why I like you guys. Everyone else in this town either looks up to criminals or looks down on anyone who isn't wealthy. You guys are bad boys, but I know you'll be good men. Except for your buddy, Ski Ski," Gordon added as a friendly warning while me, Jon, and Jeff all chuckled.

"I understand why you did what you did, but you know that's not how you're going to solve this problem," said Gordon seriously as Jon looked at me.

"We had to do something," I said nervously, remembering what Sweetheart had told me while also thinking about how the cops were now looking for us and thinking we were a gang.

57

"I know how you feel. I wanna help also. It's my job to help, but they won't let us," said Gordon.

"Who won't?" Jon replied, a confused look on his face.

"The mayor, police chief, and other cops. They are worried about the town's reputation, not to mention the rich kid's parents have too much money invested into Sunnyslope, so our chief allows them to do whatever they want. I think that's wrong, but most of the other cops would rather focus on the lower-class criminals instead. It's easier for them. We receive slightly less hate when we do," said Gordon

"What if you alone just arrest them all?" asked Jon

"I would love to throw them all in cells. I can't catch all of them myself though, and..." Gordon's face became noticeably irritated.

"Even if you did, their parents would just pay to get them out of it." I finished the sentence.

"Yes, though if I were to arrest the same dealer multiple times, maybe it wouldn't matter how much money their family has. Eventually, they would come across the wrong judge who would do the right thing and would throw them in jail. But again, I can't do it all alone, and I would probably get fired for whatever excuse they can come up with after arresting the first rich kid I found selling, seeing as the police chief seems to think more like the principal of your school. And if I only target the Northside dealers, I will get accused of discrimination for only arresting the poor kids. They want to keep it quiet to prevent panic and stop citizens from moving away."

"That's why I gathered my friends in the first place," I told him.

"I don't think this is the right way to solve this, guys. Though I don't know what to do myself, I do know that my chief told every cop to find out who attacked the dealers, and, apparently, it's a bigger priority than finding the dealers themselves. So you guys need to be careful. I suggest you find another way to help because you live on the Northside, and even when you're just skating down the street, a lot of other cops and most of the people in town target you."

"We will. I have a meeting with the mayor tomorrow, and I'll try to get his help to solve this my way," Jon said, as I looked at him and rolled my eyes. Gordon took a deep breath.

"From what I've heard, he's the one who ordered the police chief to have you guys arrested."

Jon, Jeff, and I all looked at each other in shock.

"So, the cops think catching us, who are fighting the dealers, is more important than stopping the ones who are getting everyone addicted to heroin?" I asked.

"I agree it makes no sense, but they are considering you a gang" replied Gordon

"A gang!!!?" said Jon and Jeff at the same time with a mixture of shock and anger in their voices. They both turned to me, and I nodded, confirming to them that it was true.

"I know," Gordon said,

"Crooked cops and people who abuse positions of power are just as bad as the criminals they are supposed to be stopping. I'm on your side. You guys need to know, though, that part of being an adult is understanding that not everything in our world is black and white. I think you guys are simplifying the problem. Most situations you face in life give you a choice of whether or not you wanna do the smart thing at the risk of being heartless," he said, looking at me and Jeff,

"Or do the right thing at the risk of being brainless," he continued as he looked at Jon.

"My advice to you guys is to try and find the middle ground, the gray area if you can." He finished as he shook all of our hands, this time youngest to oldest, and headed out. Jon, Jeff, and I just continued to look at each other in confusion.

What the hell is he talking about? I asked myself.

Then I asked Gordon as he was halfway out the door,

"What do you mean when you say the smart thing is heartless and the right thing is brainless?" He turned around and stepped back inside.

"Imagine you are driving through the middle of nowhere with no one around. It's so dark you can barely see anything. And then in the distance you see someone whose car broke down on the side of the road. Do you stop and help them? Or just keep driving?" Gordon asked all three of us.

"I'd stop and help them," said Jon.

"What if they are dangerous and try to kill you?" Gordon responded, his eyes on Jon, looking like he was deeply thinking about what he had just heard.

"I'd just keep driving then," said Jeff

"What if they are an innocent person and they end up dead because you didn't help them?" Gordon said to Jeff, who also seemed to be deeply contemplating.

He made a good point. I would probably just call someone and hope that a *good* cop like him showed up. That way if they were dangerous, at least the cop had a weapon. And if they weren't dangerous, they could help the person before they ended up getting hurt.

"Gordon, wait..." I said, remembering I had to give him something.

I saw in the corner of my eye that he stopped and turned around to see me walking toward my bedroom, only to return a minute later. I handed Gordon the grocery bag.

"Can you get rid of this for me before my Ma finds it and freaks out? She already hides the air freshener because she heard a story about Ski Ski inhaling it to try to get high, and for some irrational reason, she thinks I would actually do the same thing. Honestly If we didn't have so much history with Ski Ski, we wouldn't even be friends with him.

"Having a brainless friend can be just as bad as having a heartless one," said Gordon looking at the bag.

"And sadly he's both." I added slightly laughing.

Gordon's eyes widened as he looked inside the bag to find a large number of pills and other drug paraphernalia that I gathered from the dealers.

"We took everything the dealers had, but I didn't know how to properly dispose of it," I told him

"Thank you. I'll take care of it," Gordon said.

"If you just so happen to come across anymore, call me, and I'll come to get it from you. You do not want anyone catching you with this. No other cop in Sunnyslope will believe that you confiscated it from drug dealers. They will think that you are the drug dealers." Gordon smiled and left, leaving me just standing there to question what I believed.

On Thanksgiving, me, Jon, and Sweetheart woke up early and met up at the mayor's office for the appointment. I guess Sweetheart still agreed with Jon's more mature and passive approach to handling the situation. She repeatedly said to me,

"Please stop what you guys are doing." Even though all this did was agitate me, when she asked me to come with them, I couldn't say no. As soon as we sat down, we quickly understood just why the meeting was set on Thanksgiving.

"Sorry to rush you guys," the mayor said, not sounding sorry at all,

"But it is Thanksgiving, and I have to get back to my family."

I shook my head, but only Sweetheart seemed to notice, and she kicked my foot.

Jon responded,

"Oh well, we could come back tomorrow if you want."

"No, no, no," the mayor said,

"My schedule is packed, and we're here, so what can I do for you?"

Jon and Sweetheart told the mayor what was happening and explained how they thought he and others could help.

The mayor's fake smile instantly turned to a straight face. He interrupted,

"Do you three realize what would happen if all the people of this town knew that not only are kids becoming drug addicts but that it's also kids from this town who are selling them drugs?"

"Yes parents would be upset, but ignoring the problem isn't gonna make it go away," Sweetheart insisted.

"But acknowledging the problem might make them *move* away," the mayor rudely replied, hardley letting her get her words out.

"Property taxes would plummet if this got out."

Sweetheart, obviously upset, looked down at her hands.

I never wanted to punch somebody so badly in my life.

"Is money more important to you than the kids overdosing on heroin?" I asked. To be honest, I was trying to make him angry, given the way he was treating us. He made eye contact with me, and it took everything I had not to look away.

"We are handling the problem. I've met with the police chief, and we're dealing with it privately. I suggest you stay out of it and keep it quiet. Now if you'll excuse me, I have to be home for dinner with my family." The mayor put his fake smile back on his face and grabbed his coat.

I could tell the other two felt discouraged as we also left to return to our families for dinner. I think they started to see why I hadn't tried to talk to any of the adults in town before gathering everybody on Halloween. I had already accurately predicted that they wouldn't have helped us. Still, both Jon and Sweetheart decided it wasn't over.

"Oh, I can't stand him," said Sweetheart, covering her face with her hands.

"Me neither," Jon agreed, shaking his head.

"I think he should get his ass kicked too," added Jeff.

"What did you guys expect? Politicians are like STDs. Some are worse than others, but they're all bad," I told them, and we all burst out laughing together.

Chapter 4

...And No Justice For All

Over the next few days, I tried to be supportive as Jon and Sweetheart brainstormed other peaceful methods to prevent drug dealing. They finally decided that if they couldn't follow through with their plan with any help, they would just find a way to do it themselves.

"If they won't help us, we'll figure it out on our own," said Sweetheart fiercely.

So, Sweetheart and Jon came up with a plan to start holding secret meetings at the church. At these meetings, Sweetheart, Jon, and anyone who showed up would discuss how they could help with the drug problem in Sunnyslope. They spread the word around town that anyone was welcome and this would be a safe place for those recovering from addiction to vent about the issues they faced. Unfortunately, only a few people showed up to the first meeting.

I didn't need to tell them that if they got caught, the mayor, the police chief, and the principal would find some way to punish them for it because, despite my friends' good intentions, the town's leaders lived in denial about how serious the problem was. I had no idea what the consequences would be.

I got an intrusive thought for a second about Sweetheart getting expelled and sent to the BD school. Then I told myself that would never happen. She was a straight A student who never ditched class. Her parents were too wealthy and connected to let that happen, which was a relief, at least until I thought about my friends and I getting expelled for what we were doing.

I respected and supported what both Jon and Sweetheart were trying to do and thought that helping addicts was a great idea, and I wished Zero were able to receive their help. I stopped by a meeting or two, and I liked the fact that addicts left the meeting feeling noticeably better.

However, I still believed we needed to start at the source. There would be no need for meetings and raising awareness if there were no drug dealers to begin with, and I wasn't willing to wait until after they became addicted to help those people. I didn't even want to bother trying to convince kids not to turn to drugs for their problems or for fun, especially when most of them thought it was cool. Knowledge paled in comparison to wisdom. Knowledge was being told, and wisdom was being shown. I wanted to prevent the opportunity to get drugs, so these idiots didn't have to learn the hard way.

"I don't know why hardly any people are showing up to our meetings," Sweetheart said.

"We're trying to help, and it seems like no one cares." I could tell she was becoming disheartened.

"Most people have selective empathy and don't care about things until it affects them personally," I told her.

"There's two types of people. There are the ones who justify the horrible things they say, do, and believe. Then there are the ones who think the horrible things they say, do, and believe are just. But neither of them will get involved in a situation until they feel like it could hurt or benefit themselves personally." I felt sad as I said it.

"Well I'm not gonna be one of those people" Sweetheart said feistily.

"I know," I grinned, feeling a quick burst of happiness as I stared at her while she, thankfully, wasn't looking. Even though we agreed to disagree, the fact that Sweetheart was, as usual, so caring and determined to help people, while at the same time using a very logical approach, reminded me why I liked her so much. We would eventually see who was right.

Over the next couple of weeks, I continued to make an appearance in order to demonstrate my support for Jon's and Sweetheart's efforts. I didn't talk, but I felt that just being there showed that I cared. They held meetings once a week and discussed ways to help with the drug epidemic.

Meanwhile, Sweetheart and Jon kept running into the same roadblocks with the town leaders, their ideas continuing to be shut down. The principal refused to hold an assembly so they could speak to all of the students at Sunnyslope High. The mayor refused to talk to the parents of Sunnyslope. Moreover, when they tried to tell the police chief about Chronic, he told them,

"Stay out of it. We will handle it!"

It seemed no matter what plans they came up with, Sweetheart and Jon were denied permission, and no further action was being taken. Jon became angry about not receiving any help.

"God, they are such scumbags. They aren't doing anything but hoping that it'll eventually just stop. We'll just do it without their help then." He decided that they would just continue to move forward without permission.

I think they were realizing that I was at least right about one thing. We are all gonna have to risk getting into trouble to actually make a difference. Sweetheart, always the rule follower, wasn't too happy about that.

"I hope we don't get into too much trouble if they find out that we continued to try and do something," she said, worried.

"I wouldn't worry about it," I tried to reassure her.

"I don't think there's much they can do to you guys, even if they find out. Jon and them aren't in school anymore, and too many people love you too much to let anything happen to you." She smiled and put her head on my arm.

Jon and Sweetheart claimed social media would probably be the quickest and most noticeable way to inform everyone about what was happening. The best part was that they wouldn't have to worry about any interference, since there was little to nothing the mayor and the others could do to stop them, as they had no control over what they could post, not to mention they could do it anonymously.

Sweetheart showed me the page they started on a very popular social media platform. The page detailed the drug problem in Sunnyslope and had an announcement about weekly support meetings for addicts at the church. I saw that it was being shared around by a few people, and it didn't take long before everyone in town finally found out about what was going on in Sunnyslope. Still, the response wasn't exactly what they were hoping for.

Once all of the citizens, especially the parents, of Sunnyslope finally realized that there was a drug problem in town, the outrage was so overwhelming that the mayor had no choice but to call a town meeting. The outrage started online, and I saw comments saying awful things to each other. I even saw other comments that said the epidemic was all just a hoax.

Morons. All of them, I swear. I'm starting to see why supervillains wanna end the world so much, I said to myself, shaking my head to get the thoughts out as I started to question the difference between a hero and a villain.

69

The meeting was held at Sunnyslope High, and most of the adults in town showed up. This was one of those times where I was actually happy to be the quiet one in the back of the room. I stood in the corner of the Field House, the same building in which my P.E. class sometimes took place. The lower, middle, and upper classes all took turns blaming each other. They all decided to focus on certain types of people as they went back and forth.

"See I told you," one guy said,

"This town wasn't what we thought it was."

"I can't believe this. Sunnyslope was such a nice old-fashioned town," a bitter woman said to an equally resentful man.

"This town was becoming so progressive and accepting towards everyone. But I'm not surprised by this given the other side of town only cares about certain people and money," said another woman.

"This is because we allow them to live here," said yet another attendee at the meeting, but I couldn't see who it was because I put my head down to hide my laughter. It really wasn't funny, but I had to hide my face as they all started pointing the finger at every different group of people. Even the cops, teachers, and parents were being blamed. It was so foolish, it was almost comedic.

I thought to myself about how they were all willingly ignoring what was right in front of them. It was not only immoral to pretend that certain types of people were causing what was wrong in the world, but it was also unintelligent, seeing as you're more likely to be victimized by your group than any other, as they are the ones you spent the most time with. Pretending they could drop their guard around "their kind," whatever that may be, just meant that they were more likely to be targeted by them.

At least that's what I was starting to realize. To me, the transition from childhood into adulthood felt like somehow awaking in an alternate universe where there was no such thing as an adult. I had wrongly assumed as a child that most adults understood what was right and what was wrong and that they chose to do the right thing. In reality, the world was filled with people who villainized others for not caring about certain issues as much as they did, despite the fact that they didn't show any more compassion. These people made me feel normal.

This world is crazier than I am, I thought as I looked around at everyone.

I could tell by the smiles on their faces and the whispering amongst themselves that the mayor, the principal, and the police chief had a plan and that they decided to put that plan into place. They knew just how to get everyone on the same side and, more importantly, how to completely avoid any blame for Sunnyslope's drug problem.

The mayor began,

"I'm sure by now you've heard about the drug problem in our town, and just when we thought it couldn't get any worse, we find out that members of a gang of youths operating like an organized crime family are not only the ones selling the drugs, but they are also attacking the kids who bravely say no to them. All of this was just brought to my attention a couple of days ago by our police chief, and I wanted to call this meeting so we as a community can put a stop to it. It doesn't matter which class you are in, what part of town you're from, or what you look like. All the things that separate us, they don't matter. There's only one specific group of people who do things like this, and those are the sick kids who use undiagnosed mental illnesses to hide behind awful behavior. It's those kids who need to be punished."

Almost the entire crowd started cheering. Except for a very few who must not have agreed.

"Oh you son of a bit..." I started to say, feeling punched in the stomach, but I was interrupted as he continued to manipulate almost everybody.

"And luckily for us," the mayor continued,

"We now know just who those kids are because they have a hallway at the high school just for them. Some of the Behavioral Disordered kids are the ones that are responsible for both selling the drugs and attacking anyone who doesn't take them. Now please listen. It's not all of them. I wanna be clear, it's not fair to judge all of them. A few of these kids just have some issues and need a little extra help. But the other ones need to be stopped.

We have all seen them around town riding their skateboards, vandalizing stuff, starting fights, and harassing people everywhere they go. I have had numerous private discussions with the principal of Sunnyslope High about what we can do about these hooligans, and she has assured me that she put all the deans, teachers, and hall monitors on high alert so we can get these punks." The cheering continued.

"Now I can understand if you as parents would like to move to another neighborhood for the sake of your children, and it appears some already have. I hate to say it, though, those parents are cowards. This is our town, and if anyone's gonna leave, it'll be them. I also want to remind you that these crooks are everywhere, and it won't be long before your next neighborhood will end up having the same issues. I have also spoken with all of Sunnyslope's finest, who have been working discreetly day and night in an attempt to not tip them off. They are now aware of who exactly the problem is, and they assure me that they are going to be patrolling the streets night and day to try and find them so that they can put a stop to all of this." One more round of applause rang out as the mayor shook hands with the principal and the police chief, all of them smiling and posing for pictures.

The next day at the skatepark, after having heard what had happened at the meeting, the rest of the Group was just as pissed and shocked as I was about everything the mayor said.

"Wait, so they're blaming us?" asked Chish in disbelief.

"Yeah, he brought everybody together by blaming us," I said, the anger I'd been feeling for a while now beginning to swell as I thought more about it.

"The enemy of my enemy," I added.

"We gotta be even more careful now, not only you four at school…" Jon said, looking at me, D, Chish, and Ski Ski, the only ones still in high school.

"But also the rest of us. Even if we're just skating to the Skatepark or just driving to get something to eat Uptown, we have to watch out. Everyone is gonna be looking for us."

"Well that's nothing new," said Anthony, and everyone chuckled

"Jon's right. It's gonna be even worse now," said Andy.

We all agreed that Jon was right, and so we decided to be more cautious from then on. I thought about what that would look like. We would have to avoid as many people in town as possible, which wasn't much of a change for me, but for the rest of the group it was.

Also, it worried me when the mayor said that the principal and everyone at school was now involved. For us still in school, I didn't want all of this to get in the way of us graduating at the end of the school year. The problem we faced outside of school going forward was that while the cops were cruising the streets looking for the BD kids, the actual dealers were getting away with selling drugs right in front of them. At least the rich ones did; the cops actually had started to arrest some of the dealers, though it was only a few poor ones, and most of which were minorities. Some people took that as a sign of things getting better, which was exactly what the mayor wanted, to convince people that things would get better in no time.

Yet, when the cops started to get accused of discrimination, the BD kids did as well. Even though we attacked all of the dealers, we were, as usual, being targeted by both sides. So, while one side of town called us a gang, the people on the other side of the town began manipulating others into thinking we were a hate group that discriminated against only certain people. I even saw headlines on a social media article that said, "Local gang still selling drugs".

"Unbelievable," I muttered as I ripped down a sign off the bulletin board at school after noticing the giant "BD" on it that read, "Bigotry and Discrimination aren't welcome here."

Mid-December came around. After a long week of finals, Christmas Break would finally begin, which was great news for most of the BD kids that remained in school. We would have two weeks off! Rather than looking forward to the end of the semester, however, I found myself dreading it. Not only was I getting extremely anxious about whether or not I would graduate, but I also imagined that sooner or later things would be worse for us at school. I couldn't remember how many out-of-school suspensions I'd had, but if any of us got more than ten, we got expelled and sent to the BD school.

My mind raced as I walked past Sweetheart's class to see her, even if it was just the back of her head. Then I roamed the hallways to avoid going back to class.

I refuse to go to that school! I won't. Maybe I should start looking into the GED process just in case. No! That won't happen. We will all be fine. If things weren't always as good as I sometimes thought they were, then, at other times, they couldn't always be as bad. Right?

Something else was also bothering me. Chish's older brother, Greg, had in the past four years dropped out of high school and gotten his GED, and he had also battled a heroin addiction just like Zero had. He was still struggling with it, so their mom planned to move the family to a different town where he didn't know anybody and where he couldn't get drugs so easily. It was the only thing left that she could think of to save his life, but that also meant Chish would have to start at a new school for the final semester of his senior year, and he would be away from his two best friends, me and D. From now on he would have to take the train for forty-five minutes to get to Sunnyslope from his new town to visit us on the weekends.

Losing all my friends and finishing my senior year alone would be worse than all of us getting expelled.

What if he and I stopped being friends? What if he couldn't make any friends at his new school? I remembered when I had to eat lunch alone, or when I had stressed over who I could partner with in a class. What it was like before I met them or whenever my friends weren't around. Feeling emotional about Chish's move, I prayed that Ski Ski, D, and especially Sweetheart wouldn't leave too.

I struggled to take a deep breath after I finished my last final. Consequences to what we were doing, the thing I had been worried about since Halloween, were starting to happen, just as I foreseen.

I tried to look on the bright side. I had two weeks free from school and therefore, a lot more free time to find out more about who Chronic was, where we could find him, and how to stop him. Looking on the bright side only helped me for about a minute or two, though.

I headed home and waited for everyone else to finish their finals or get off work. I went for a long walk and thought about all the good times I'd had with the people I cared about, about all the dreams I wanted to make a reality. All while trying to ignore the intrusive thoughts constantly surrounding me.

To try to take my mind away from all the negative thoughts, I decided to walk past Chish's old house and go down memory lane. I stopped by my best friend's now empty house and just stared at it for a few minutes. Then I looked around the block and somehow felt even worse, quickly realizing Chish's family wasn't the only family who had moved. Other houses had for sale signs in their front yards, and I had a feeling that even more people were gonna leave Sunnyslope soon if the drug problem didn't start getting better. Naturally, some of the wealthier families could just pack up and move, but that wasn't an option for the lower-income and middle-class families. Either way, the towns they ended up moving to would just eventually end up with the same problem.

Feeling empty and hopeless, I looked towards the abandoned mansion next door. I started to get emotional about all of it and decided that the whole Group could use some fun right now. The problem, though, was that we could rarely skate in the winter because of how cold it got and how often it snowed in Chicago.

Then, looking at the unnecessarily big house next door to Chish's, I came up with an idea. I remembered an episode from one of my favorite TV shows growing up where the main character built an indoor skatepark inside his house while his parents were out of town. If we could find everything we needed, I thought, we could do the same thing in one of the empty homes!

The Group loved my idea. It took a couple of days of sneaking around at night, but we were able to steal some wood from a construction site.

"Why didn't we think of this sooner?" asked D, carrying one corner of a large stack of wood.

"Yeah. Now we have a place to hang out and our own skatepark," said Jeff, even more excited than me, walking behind us as he struggled to carry five skateboards.

"I hope we don't get caught. I'm sure the cops would love to arrest us for breaking and entering," Jon said as he carried another corner of the stack.

"Don't break or ruin anything in there, guys," he added.

"Seriously."

"We won't," I said, also helping with the wood.

"Why? It's not like we'll have to pay for it?" said Jeff.

"It doesn't matter, it's still wrong. Just don't destroy anything," Jon said firmly.

"Dude! A car is coming. Let's go over here," said Sarge, carrying the last corner and leading us all out of the sight. We hoped they didn't see us and hoped even more that the driver wasn't a cop.

We started with a mini ramp and then built a box. Then we gathered some extra furniture from our homes and bought some Christmas lights to light up the pitch black inside. The Group spent every day at the big beautiful house. We even met up on Christmas Eve after having dinner with our families. We had a blast every time I got all of my friends together to hang out in the house.We had managed to create the perfect sanctuary to skate in during the winter. I realized we could also use it as a lookout to plan and discuss the ongoing fight against the dealers and the search for Chronic. I felt like our efforts to help the drug problem were slowly but surely paying off, and we were actually starting to accomplish our goal.

We had a small party on New Year's Eve. We got some food, listened to music, skated in the house on the ramps we had made. We also took turns going out on patrol. We split up into small groups and went looking for dealers before coming back and having some fun.

Going out on patrol and finding dealers had actually become a daily thing at this point. Sweetheart, who had to be convinced to enter the empty home to begin with, gave me a dirty look every time any of us went out, making it obvious how she felt about what we were doing! I would just playfully look back at her or respond to whatever she said with a witty remark.

Sweetheart was more critical than usual, and I assumed it was because she just wanted to enjoy the New Year.

"You just got back not too long ago, Jay. That's enough. Please stop, you don't need to go out and find any more tonight," she said.

"I'm sure that's the same thing the family and friends of drug addicts say before the dealers kill them," I said the second she stopped talking. Then I followed Jon and Anthony outside. I didn't see her facial expression, but I knew my quick witty comments either made her laugh, drove her crazy, annoyed her, or did all of those things. So, when we got back I knew there was a fifty-fifty chance of her being in a good mood or being pissed off.

Between the good times I was having with my friends and the feeling that we were making a difference, I became a little more optimistic about things. I was taking all of my anxieties, depression, and guilt out on the dealers, which helped me feel accomplished. Yes, people were still using and overdosing, but I could see it happening slightly less, which, to me, meant we were slowly solving the problem. With every fight and with each batch of drugs we collected, I felt a little of my rage slowly start to disappear.

To a seventeen-year-old who loved superheroes, it seemed like the problem in Sunnyslope was an easy fix. We couldn't make people choose to stop selling drugs, but we could punish them for it, while also preventing as many addicts as possible from getting their hands on the drugs. As long as we continued to do that, I believed that eventually no one else would become addicted or die of an overdose. I wasn't as mature as Jon or Sweetheart, but everyone kept telling me that issues like these weren't easy fixes, that it wasn't just about taking action, it was about taking the right action., which is exactly what I thought I was doing.

The next night, after their patrol duty, D and Colin walked back into the house by themselves. Sarge wasn't with them, strange given that he had left with them to go hunting.

"Where's Sarge at?" I asked them.

"He ran home really quick," D told me.

"He said he'd be right back," Colin added.

"Oh, okay," I replied.

When Sarge did finally show up, he was gushing blood from his nose.

"What the hell happened to you?" I asked.

"Some other skaters jumped me and told me to stop selling drugs in their town," he told us.

"Dude, I've never been so pissed off in my life!"

Furious, we all swiftly set out to get revenge.

"Let's go find them right now," said Jon after seeing his friend's injuries.

Sweetheart pleaded for us not to retaliate.

"They are just trying to do the same thing you guys are. Everyone thinks you're the ones selling drugs, remember? Don't do this. They aren't dealers."

Her words, however, only made us want to get them even more. When we arrived at the scene of Sarge's fight, the other group was already gone. Just knowing they were attacking the wrong people made us even angrier at them. So we made it a point to find them and make them pay.

After the holidays, Jon and Sweetheart tried to continue holding their meetings at the church, though I noticed even fewer and fewer people showed up at each meeting. With everything going on, tensions started rising even more between Jon, Jeff, and I. We were all constantly short with each other. Especially me and Jon. He still didn't like what we were doing, and I was also pissed, since, clearly, his plan wasn't helping either, and yet he was still so critical of everything I did. Or arguments became more frequent than usual.

"We need to stop attacking the dealers," Jon said angrily.

"It's only making things worse."

"Things only got worse when you told an entire town filled with complete morons about what was happening," I responded bitterly

"You're both morons. Now shut the hell up or I'm gonna hit both of you," said Jeff, also mad since everything he said from the start was either ignored or shot down.

"Gordon's right," said Jon coldly.

"You're a heartless jerk."

"And you're a brainless bitch," I shook in anger.

Jon punched me in the chin, and I think we were both shocked it didn't knock me out cold. I saw stars for a second, then to both of our surprise, I actually hit him back for once, though not nearly as hard as he hit me. Growing up, I could never actually throw a real punch at someone I cared about, knowing I would feel horrible if I did. I did feel bad later but for not as long as I used to, which was abnormal for me. I started to wonder if I was becoming colder or more confident. Jeff, who normally got in between us to prevent a fight, tackled both of us to the ground and punched each of us in the face while me and Jon continued to exchange blows and focus on each other.

Colin, Andy and Sarge also attempted to break it up. Sarge grabbed me, Andy grabbed Jeff, and Colin grabbed Jon before we could do any more damage to each other. I didn't care if Jon had a problem with what we were doing; every time someone else came up with another plan it failed, only making me feel more confident that I was doing the right thing. It's just like when a superhero gets looked at as the bad guy by everyone, even though the hero is the one making a difference. They would all see that I was right, that I was the only one who had actually come up with a working plan. Just when I started to think I had everything figured out though, the cops in town started to close in on us.

Chapter 5

Renegade Romance

"**D**on't lose the dealers, Ant!" I yelled to Anthony. He was running faster than the rest of us.

"I'm gonna catch you eventually, so you might as well stop!" said Anthony, and I laughed. We turned a street corner to see the Southside dealers we were chasing, now walking casually, to our surprise, until we noticed who they were waving to.

"It's the cops! Go!" yelled Anthony, and we all took off running. As it turned out, the group and I spent all of February running. In addition to chasing the dealers, skating all over town meant we were also constantly running from the cops. The harassment we faced was now almost daily.

"It's bad enough that they aren't arresting half of the dealers," I told Chish on the phone one day to catch him up on what'd been going on since he moved.

"But now they are getting in the way of us stopping the half they aren't arresting."

The only time we didn't have to deal with the crooked cops was when we were at home, at school, or in the abandoned mansion we now called The Lookout. I was worried about what would happen if we got arrested. They might catch up to us eventually, but to be honest, all of this running from the cops was kinda thrilling. I could tell that I wasn't the only one who felt this way either. It seemed to me that all of the Group enjoyed the fact that they never caught us.

"Once we can start skating outside again, they're never gonna catch us whether it's in their cars...or on foot," Andy said, and our laughs all echoed throughout the Lookout.

As spring approached, the Group was excited to finally start going to the skatepark again. This was another place where we most likely wouldn't have to deal with any cops or most of Sunnyslope. The skatepark was like the BD hallway for when we were outside of school. Another home away from home.

After the new semester began Ski Ski, D, and I seemed to get in trouble on a more regular basis, and we started receiving more punishments at school than usual. The number of lunch detentions and in-school suspensions stemming from ditching and being constantly late for classes had already doubled from the previous semester. We normally ditched or were late, but now that we were on the hunt for dealers, we were tardy even more often.. I became more anxious knowing that the out-of-school suspensions were coming next, and I was extremely stressed at the thought of all three of us getting expelled before we had a chance to graduate.

What are we gonna do if we get expelled? I'll end up dropping out just like Zero did. All the help I received from my Ma, Sweetheart, my counselor, and my teachers will have been for nothing. There are a lot of drug dealers at that school. What if they recognize us or know who we are? We'll be surrounded.

I shook my head violently to get rid of the negative thoughts of Ski Ski, D, or even myself ending up like Zero. However, I spent the next few weeks in a constant state of stress, and I started to seriously wonder whether or not we could keep doing this without all of us messing up our personal lives in the process.

The month of March was an exciting time for the Group. Spring had arrived, which meant two things: The skate park finally reopened, and Saint Paddy's Day was coming up. Saint Patrick's Day was a big deal in Sunnyslope. Chicago and some of its suburbs are known for going all out for the holiday, and every year there was a parade on the Southside of town the Saturday afternoon one week prior to the parade held in the city.

I wasn't as excited for this event as I normally was. In fact, I felt chest pains from the stress of knowing there would not only be dealers there, but also most of the cops in Sunnyslope would be there as well. I was positive they would be looking for us too.

The skatepark reopened a few days before the parade, and D, Ski Ski, and I all talked about heading there right after school.

"It's so nice out. I wanna go and skate so bad," I told D and Ski Ski

"Let's do it." said Ski Ski

"Yeah, let's go to the skatepark right after school," said D.

"I might go right now and just ditch eighth period," I told them

"I can't today," said Ski Ski

"Yeah me neither. I have to make up a test, " said D.

"We'll just meet you there after school," Ski Ski added.

"Sounds good," I told them as they walked to class.

For a second, I worried about ditching since I had been getting into more and more trouble, but I told myself that it was fine. I still hadn't gotten into as much trouble as Ski Ski and D had lately. Sweetheart was always a good motivator for me to behave, but she got out of school after sixth period, so she was already gone for the day. I just hoped she or my Ma wouldn't find out about it. It was seventy degrees out and a little windy, so I was so excited when I walked out of the Ditch Door and hopped on my skateboard. I skated so fast that I got to the skatepark in half the time it would normally take me to get there.

Jon and Sarge pulled up just as I rolled into the parking lot.

"What's up?" I asked, smiling. We talked for a few seconds before heading in.

"Aren't you supposed to be in school still?" asked Jon.

"I've been good lately, so I decided to reward myself," I told him. He shook his head while Sarge laughed. Then Sarge suddenly switched to an expression of anger, shaking his head left and right.

"What's wrong?" I asked, following his gaze towards the skatepark.

"Dude, those are the guys," he said. Both Jon and I stood in confusion. Then it hit me.

"The skaters who jumped you?" I asked. I was already getting pissed off.

"How many of them are there?" Jon asked him.

Sarge looked around the park.

"Looks like five of them."

"I'll call Anthony and Colin so it'll be an even fight," Jon said, putting his glass bottle of iced tea into his other hand. Then he pulled out his phone and took a few steps away from us to be able to hear.

Sarge and I talked about what we wanted to do. I decided to call D and Ski Ski, since I knew they would probably be out of school and on their way here already.

"Yo, what's up?" said D.

"Hey where are you guys at?" I asked. Surprised I didn't get his voicemail.

"Ummm. I don't know," he said.

"About three minutes. Maybe five. We asked to go to the bathroom and just left school. Why what's up?" I told him to hurry and informed him of what was going on. I was glad that they were so close, since Jon said that Anthony and Colin wouldn't be here for another ten minutes.

When Ski Ski and D skated up, we didn't even greet each other. We all just headed towards the skatepark, ready to get revenge. Walking inside, Sarge asked the dealers,

"Do you remember me?"

"Yeah," one of them responded.

"You guys are the ones selling heroin to everybody," he said as his friends. seeming nervous, joined his side. Clearly, they weren't expecting a fight.

"We're not the ones selling heroin," Jon said sternly.

"We're the ones trying to *stop* the people who are selling it."

"Yeah, sure," one of the other skaters said sarcastically.

"I don't care what you idiots think," I said. My fingers hurt from clenching my fist so tightly.

"You jumped our friend. So I hope that you enjoyed skating while you could because you're not gonna be skating again for a while."

"You guys couldn't have even given him a fair fight?" asked Jon, also furious.

"We don't wanna fight. We came here to skate, man," one of them said, his eyes wide appearing more and more nervous. Sarge didn't back down.

"We'll give you a choice even though you didn't give me one. You fight me one on one, or we can all fight five on five? I'd prefer one on one."

The other skaters stuttered with their words as they tried to plead with us. This continued until the head skater, the one we had approached, yelled to his friends,

"Run!"

They all tried to run away, but Ski Ski managed to tackle the largest one to the ground. Somehow, though, he got on top of Ski Ski. I heard breaking glass as D and I started kicking him Turns out, Jon had hit him in the head with his drink to get him off of Ski Ski. The other four turned around and came back to help the friend we had caught but only just to join their friend on the ground.

Finally, we heard someone yell,

"Break it up!" A parent was running over from the playground next to the skate park. Next thing we knw, we heard sirens. Everyone turned their heads in the same direction as the sound of the sirens became closer, and then we all took off running towards the parking lot. Fortunately, we got there first since the other skaters were slow to get up. The BD kids all jumped into Jon's car, and he peeled off, going the wrong way down a one-way street, a smart move since the cops pulled into the parking lot just as we got away. We had hoped we drove off in time before anyone could get Jon's license plate number.

"We need to call Colin and Anthony and tell them not to go to the skatepark," I told Jon, the adrenaline still running through me.

"Oh yeah, you're right." Jon pulled out his phone at the next stop sign.

From what he told me, Anthony and Colin showed up at the skatepark and pulled in right behind the cops. I never felt more satisfied than I did when I heard that not only did Colin and Anthony drive away without the cops even noticing them, but all the other skaters got caught, and the ones that weren't taken to the hospital were arrested. Thankfully, none of them were too banged up. We were worried about the guy Jon had hit with a glass bottle. I mean we didn't want to really hurt anyone that badly. He had just gotten caught up in the moment, and his instinct to protect our friends had taken over. I was actually surprised Jon did that. I guess he was feeling a similar rage to what I had been feeling.

Then suddenly my satisfaction turned to a surge of pure terror.

If someone as humble as Jon is capable of losing himself for a second, then it's only a matter of time before I become the person that my intrusive thoughts make me think I am. I'll stop myself if I have to. I won't let myself become a monster. Fighting drug dealers is one thing, but I don't want to hurt anyone.

On the day of the parade, I woke up to hear someone saying my name.

"Dammit, Jason, wake the hell up." I looked around to see Andy sitting on my bed, which instantly drove me crazy. I hated anyone other than me sitting or laying on my bed. I also saw Jon, fully dressed and trying to wake up Jeff who was still passed out on his bed.

"The parade starts in a few minutes. Me and Andy are gonna be outside so hurry up," he said

"And don't go back to sleep. Or were leaving without you," Andy added with a smile as he threw a pillow at me.

As Andy and Jon walked outside, Jeff finally woke up and quickly shot out of bed and put on his pants, his tongue again resting across his cheek like a happy puppy. We were running late already. The main road that took us to the end of the parade was blocked off by the parade itself, and the sidewalks were so crowded, it was a challenge for us to get to the main area where the rest of our friends had gathered.

"The parade is gonna be over by the time we make it through all of these people," Jon complained.

"Well if Jay and Jeff didn't sleep in so late…" Andy joked,

"We could've been there before it got all crowded."

"Maybe we can just skate down a side street to get there faster," I told them. Then we saw Jeff just jump on his skateboard and started sketching alongside one of the vehicles in the parade.

"Jeff!" hollered me and Jon at the same time, thinking he was gonna get hurt or in trouble.

"Let's go," said Andy, laughing as he followed in Jeff's lead. Me and Jon looked at each other for a few seconds and then shrugged before deciding to do the same.

As we skated between the crowds of people, we noticed that some of the signs and shirts people wore weren't the usual Irish pride signs.

"Do you see the signs?" I asked Jon, and we all looked around to see that some of the citizens of Sunnyslope were using the holiday to protest the BD kids. Some of the Southsiders' signs said, "Gangs are not welcome in Sunnyslope." Meanwhile, the Northsiders had signs that read, "Hate doesn't have a home here." We also saw shirts that said, "BD are snitches."

"Yeah," Jon shook his head.

Idiots. I said to myself. Even worse, the Northsiders had the nerve to try to pass selling drugs off as a mental health issue.

I come from a family of gangsters, and substance abusers, and I'm severely mentally ill. And I've never sold or tried drugs. They are all pathetic. How inherently stupid or poorly raised do you have to be to wanna be a part of either side? I shook my head.

We were given dirty looks by almost everybody, just for having skateboards. I could tell by the way spectators looked down at them. The fact that we were skating through the parade probably didn't help. I was baffled by the hypocrisy and ignorance of people on both sides of town. The same people who had made us always feel unwelcome in Sunnyslope were now treating us like we were the ignorant ones.

The Southsiders looked down on us, still implying that we were all drug addicts or selling drugs. Meanwhile, the Northsiders still mocked us because we didn't take or sell drugs, accusing us of being cowards. It was shocking that both sides of town thought they were better when both were so awful.

I think most political issues are like incomplete math equations, and political people are like children trying to solve those incomplete equations. Everyone is usually biasly guessing but acting like their opinions are facts. The average person apparently can't tell the difference between progression and escalation. Politics makes good people look evil. Evil people look good. Smart people look stupid. Stupid people look smart. Enemies look like friends, and friends look like enemies. We were helping all of them, but they treated us like we were the problem. Most of them didn't even deserve our help.

Maybe we're wrong for getting in the way of people dealing with the consequences of their own actions. Maybe we're just enabling everybody to continue to do what they are doing. It's the repercussions of an action that shows you whether you are right or wrong. What if no one is learning anything because there's always someone else to deal with their problems?" I shook my head, trying to focus on moving forward while skating through the parade.

A few minutes later we arrived at the Seven-Eleven, and we met up with Ski Ski, Chish, D, Colin, Sarge, and Anthony. Unfortunately, Sweetheart had to stay away from us at the parade. Her parents were there and still hated me and my friends.

"Okay sooo," Colin said to the Group as we greeted each other.

"I asked around and heard of a few dealers that will be trying to sell during the parade. I just don't know where yet."

We decided to split up and started looking around, figuring they would've found a place away from the crowd. We searched the whole surrounding area, and just as I decided to head back to the Seven-Eleven, I got a call from Ski Ski.

"Dude! I found some. Come to the back of Seven Eleven," he said.

"Okay, I'll be right there," I responded before hanging up my phone.

I rushed away from the parade and over to the 7-11, where I found Jon already there, standing across from six dealers, pleading with them to stop what they were doing. Unsurprisingly, these specific dealers were Southsiders. You could tell they were jocks just by the tacky way they dressed. It made sense that the Northside dealers wouldn't risk selling on the Southside. Even if everyone was focused on the BD kids, they were still a part of the lower class, and also were, therefore, looked down upon and more likely to be targeted by cops as well.

It was obvious the dealers were about to jump us, as they were looking around, presumably to make sure no one else was around to witness. However, just as the dealers appeared to get ready to attack us, a loud commanding voice yelled,

"Freeze!"

We turned around to see a swarm of police officers, one of them aggressively holding Ski Ski by his arm. I was surprisingly glad to see the cops, for they had unintentionally stopped us from being jumped by the dealers. Yet, that relief quickly transformed into fury, as the dealers also looked at the cops and one of the poorly dressed dealers told them,

"These guys just tried to sell us drugs."

"Oh, you scumbag," I said. Now, we were going to be the ones getting arrested.

"Get on the ground now!" one of the cops screamed at Jon. I looked around, hoping that Gordon was amongst the rest of the cops, but he wasn't with them. Shocked and angry, the two of us looked at each other, then at Ski Ski. None of us needed to say it, but we all knew what we needed to do.

In the blink of an eye, Ski Ski yanked his arm away from the cop who held him, and all three of us took off running. We could hear the cops follow after us, and I looked back in a rage to see the dealers escaping. We ran through the crowds to lose the cops, but it didn't work, as the crowd also slowed us down. So we decided to just head for a side street and hop on our skateboards. We heard the cop's radio go off as they requested backup,

"They are running down the side street! Cut them off!" yelled one of the cops.

"Cut through one of the houses!" I tried to say loud enough so that Jon and Ski Ski could hear me but not so loud that the cops would. We managed to avoid getting cut off but only after the cops requested backup. Almost every cop in town was chasing us throughout the neighborhood.

The chase lasted hours. We ran through backyards and hid in bushes until the sun set and the parade had been long over. At that point, the three of us were exhausted and covered in dirt, sweat, and cuts from the branches that scraped us as we jumped in and out of trees and bushes.

"We have to find somewhere to hide out for the night," Jon gasped, trying to catch his breath. I knew he meant a place where we could go to get off the streets. We all ducked when a searchlight passed through the bushes.

"The Lookout is the closest place that I can think of, " I said, breathing heavily, so worried and so tired that I could fall asleep on somebody's front lawn right then

"Sounds good." Jon agreed.

"Let's head there," Ski Ski nodded in agreement from the hunched position he was in after he threw up. Fortunately for the three of us, not *all* the cops in Sunnyslope recognized us, and it seemed they weren't able to match our faces to our names yet. We had the confidence that we could get away without the cops showing up at one of our houses. As long as they didn't catch one of us now.

"We should order a pizza when we get there," I said. My stomach was growling.

"Hell yeah!" Ski Ski added with excitement.

"Sounds good to me" said Jon as we all kept running.

I guess as the three of us were running from the cops, the rest of the Group got my text letting them know the cops were after us and that the dealers got away. Sarge texted me back to tell me they decided to go track down the actual dealers and get their supply and revenge for them blaming us for selling. Colin knew a few people around town who also hated the dealers because they either lost someone or struggled with addictions themselves. He asked them where those specific dealers might be after the parade. He was able to find out where the six of them had gone and managed to track them down to the local college, Sunnyslope University.

Andy texted Jon to say:

Me, Colin, Anthony, Sarge, D, Chish, and Jeff caught up to the dealers who were selling at a college party, and we got them. After the six vs six fight NOT including Jeff, haha. We grabbed any drugs we could find from the dealers and the buyers so we could give it all to Gordon. We didn't even have to worry about any of the other cops showing up since every cop in town was looking for you guys haha. We were able to do what we came to do and leave without any other problems.

As Jon, Ski Ski approached the Lookout, we were able to breathe a sigh of relief for a second. We would be safe soon. I was so anxious to get there so we could all finally let our guard down and feel safe.

"Oh, finally!" said Ski Ski when the mansion was only a few houses away. I wiped the sweat off my forehead in pure relief. Yet, as fast as it came, I felt all of that hope completely drain away when I saw the terrifying familiar glow of red and blue lights reflecting off of all the windows on the block as multiple squad cars pulled up and surrounded us.

"Oh, shit," mumbled Jon and I simultaneously, knowing that there was nowhere left to run. We were caught.

Jon and I kept quiet as we were handcuffed and placed into the back of one of the squad cars. Ski Ski wasn't as smart. Instead of just keeping his mouth shut, he decided to insult them. One of the cops slammed him onto the trunk of the car and then bounced his head off of it. Ski Ski yelled,

"This is police brutality!" Then nothing but muffled words and choking sounds came out of his mouth as the cop stuck his fingers in Ski Ski's mouth, presumably to prevent him from saying anything.

Jon and I tried to get out to help our friend, forgetting we were in handcuffs and locked inside the cop car. We quickly realized that we were trapped and yelled at the crooked cop attacking Ski Ski.

"Stop it! He's just a kid!" said Jon angry

"That's enough! Leave him alone!" I pleaded with them, but there was no use. All we could do was watch as the cop repeatedly attacked our friend and wait for it to be over, all the while wondering if we would be next.

A few hours later, my Ma, furious, had to pick us up, yet again, from the police station. This time, to our relief, her anger was more directed towards the cops when she found out that not only had they attacked Ski Ski, but they had also broken Ski Ski's arm. My Ma wanted to press charges on the cop who did it, but since Ski Ski wasn't her son legally, and they didn't break mine or Jon's arm, there wasn't much she could do but hope that Ski Ski's mom would get a lawyer.

"Maybe we should just move to a new town," Ma said.

"There are kids selling drugs, kids doing drugs, and my kids are being accused of doing all of it. I'm sick of these cops, and that mayor." She was fed up with everything that's happened ever since Zero passed.

"We can't do that," Jon said.

"Most of our friends are still here," I added, thinking about all of the BD kids and Sweetheart.

"Ah... shit. We're moving?" Jeff let slip out accidentally.

"Jeffery! Watch your mouth!" my Ma said. Jon and I hid our faces and quietly chuckled.

"Well something needs to change and soon, or else we're leaving. If one of those cops had broken one of your arms, or if I was Ski Ski's mom, I would've lost it. Thank God I didn't bring your aunt or she'd be in jail right now! Ma's sister had a history of saying whatever she felt no matter how blunt she was. Jon, Jeff, and I looked at each other in concern as we thought about what it would mean for us to leave Sunnyslope and all of our friends behind.

The cops were frustrated when they didn't find any drugs on Jon, and I. Ski Ski, however, did have drugs, which made Jon, Jeff, and I even angrier. All along, we had assumed Ski Ski must have taken the dealer's stuff and was being blamed for selling the drugs.

"Gordon was right. No one believed that we confiscated it from the actual drug dealers," I said as I thought about the cast on Ski Ski's Arm.

Thankfully, we didn't also get charged with possession because Gordon vouched for us. He tried to suggest that it was the other kids who had drugs, and that we had confiscated it. Though they didn't believe it. Both Jon and I did, however, get community service and probation, and we had to pay hundreds of dollars in fines and court fees. This wasn't bad considering Ski Ski was sent to jail. Not only did he have drugs on him, but apparently all of his prior arrests for various things had piled up, and the cops lied and said that he resisted so badly he broke his own arm. So the judge decided to give him a month in jail to send a message to him and his drug dealer friends.

Jon and I were beyond pissed off that Ski Ski was in jail. We didn't have too much free time to think about it, though, since we spent most of April at the church doing our community service and dealing with the backlash of getting arrested. We actually didn't mind it. We mostly got to spend our time with our grandpa, serving food to the people who stopped by the church and teaching kids boxing, which we often did anyway. The only major issue, other than Ski Ski being locked up, was that now every single cop in Sunnyslope knew who we were and what we looked like.

Jon and I discussed the problems we would face going forward, now that we were public enemy number one. Even one of the local papers, *The Sunnyslope Independent,* had a picture of us with a caption that said, "Two of three local drug dealers not charged after arrest." Another paper said, "Corruption and privilege help drug dealers walk."

Both the Northside and the Southside of Sunnyslope all knew exactly who we were and hated us even more now, which didn't seem possible. From what I heard around school, the dealers especially hated us.

For some reason they were jealous of the negative attention we received. They thought that the reputation of a drug dealer was cool.

"Other than being hated by everyone in town except our family and friends, it's actually nice to see everybody get along for a change and agree on something," I said wittily.

"That's not funny," Jon said, irritated.

"Everyone has it out for us, including the actual drug dealers," he continued.

"We can't even leave the church or the sanctuary without a problem now. It won't be long before all of our friends and family are also singled out. This is why I didn't think this was a good idea from the start."

I put my head down, feeling guilty that everyone I cared about was now a target. Part of me just wanted to tell all of my family and friends not to go outside unless they had to.

"For now we all just have to be even more careful and lay low especially when we're out with our family and friends," I said.

"We can ask the rest of the Group to handle most of the patrolling for us until things cool down."

"That's not fair to ask them that," said Jon

"Yeah I know that Jon, but if we don't, the overdoses are gonna increase every day, just like before," I replied.

Jon still didn't agree with my approach, but he couldn't deny the fact that there were fewer cases of kids overdosing than before Halloween. Some dealers had thankfully given up the dealing because they were afraid of what would happen if we caught them selling again, and other kids were more reluctant to try the drugs after hearing about all the overdoses. This knowledge kept me going. I was doing this for Zero.

Ski Ski was released from jail a month later. As soon as he got back to school, though, things started to get bad fast for us BD kids still at Sunnyslope High. Now that Chish had moved to another town, Ski Ski, D, and Sweetheart were the only friends I had left at school.

While D, Ski Ski, and I typically got into trouble, lately we were getting into trouble a lot more than usual, and it was for things that normally wouldn't have been that big of a deal. If we ditched, made jokes in class, or swore, we automatically got sent to the L.A.C., without any warnings. The BD hallway was conveniently located right next to the Learning Adjustment Center, which was a small classroom where all students would serve both lunch detention and "in schools." The BD kids would be sent to L.A.C. whenever we misbehaved, aka most of the time. When one of us got into trouble, we would get one of three punishments for misbehaving, the least severe being lunch detention, which we would usually get for being late to the same class more than twice. Students with lunch detention would have to go straight to the L.A.C. rather than to the cafeteria.

If you got caught ditching class or had an unexcused absence, you were given an "in school," and you would be stuck in L.A.C all day rather than going to your normal eight classes. The most serious of the three was an out-of-school suspension. If you got into a fight, cursed out a teacher, or did anything more serious, you would be given an "out of School" and would either be sent home for the rest of the day or not be allowed back in school until the suspension was over.

Even though most of us BD kids preferred getting "out-of-schools," we needed to be careful now because we were getting close to the tenth suspension that would get us expelled, and I did NOT want us to get sent to the BD School.

Being in L.A.C. wasn't all bad, considering Ms. G was in charge, and Ms. G was one of the sweetest people you'd ever meet. It did raise some questions, though, as to why we were getting more severe punishments compared to the usual lunch detentions.

The best part of getting L.A.C., other than seeing Ms. G, was that if you were behind on work or had a test to make up, you could catch up on school work and homework. Sometimes, usually right before a semester was about to end, I would get L.A.C. on purpose just to catch up on all of my missing assignments and get my grades up. Also, just like when I was in class, whenever I had an in-school suspension, at least one, if not all, of my friends were usually in there with me.

One day Ski Ski, D, and I all decided to take a long lunch and ditch the class after our lunch period. We would be graduating soon, and then our days of ditching our responsibilities to go have some fun would, I imagine, happen a lot less often. We figured we could ditch one class. Our reasoning was that since Ski Ski had been in jail, he hadn't been at school to get any recent unexcused absences. Also, me and D managed to avoid ditching by getting passes out of class, so technically we didn't have any unexcused absences either. So, we figured we had a little leeway. We came in through the Ditch Door, our hair and clothes still wet from the rain, and we ran straight into a hall monitor.

"You three. Show me your hall pass," said the hall monitor.

Instead of stopping and trying to come up with some excuse, as we usually did, Ski Ski started running, causing both me and D to instinctively try to run away as well. Yet, now that we were seniors, the school didn't feel as big as it used to back during our freshman year. The hall monitors were spread out throughout the school, each carrying a walkie-talkie, and it only took about ten to fifteen minutes before we were cornered on the third floor. Even though we kinda enjoyed the game of hide and seek with all of the hall monitors, it only made our punishment worse. I was mad at Ski Ski for getting us in more trouble than we would've been if we hadn't run away.

"Why do we hang out with him again?" I asked D.

"I don't know, but now we're gonna get suspended again," D said, also pissed off.

I had hoped that maybe we could help Ski SKi become a better person someday. After all, it wasn't his fault he was raised poorly and was inherently messed up. In some ways, I think he did become a slightly better person when he was around us, or maybe he just got better at pretending to be one. Either way, the worse of a friend Ski Ski was over the years, the more my brothers and I asked ourselves at what point do we walk away from the friendship.

The constant disappointment that came from trying to help someone who would only take advantage of good-natured people, as well as the unhealthy relationship that came with it, were part of the reason I was so cold and angry towards Zero. Even though Zero and Ski Ski were exact opposites, I wrongfully projected the resentment I had obtained from Ski Ski onto Zero.

We were taken to our dean, who escorted us to the L.A.C. to remain for the rest of the day. The next day, each of us would have another out-of-school suspension for running, bringing us one step closer to being expelled.

Ms. G had a talk with us while we were in L.A.C. with her.

"The principal knows what you guys are doing with the dealers and wants all three of you expelled. He also knows that the deans, the hall monitors, and most of the teachers were told to look for any excuse they could find to suspend you. I think she, like the mayor and the police chief, wanted to avoid blame by using the BD kids as a scapegoat."

I was right. I had feared that we might not graduate before getting expelled, and now it seemed like that fear was becoming a reality.

"She wants you guys expelled and sent to the BD school, so they can pretend progress is being made with the drug problem," said Ms. G, a sad look on her face. She always told us not to get into too much trouble, that we didn't belong at that school. I could also tell by the empathetic way she was acting and talking that she felt we shouldn't be getting as much hate from everyone. She must have known that all we were trying to do was help in response to what had happened to Zero.

Zero was one of Ms. G's favorite students. I could tell by the tears in her eyes that she had been genuinely upset when she had heard that he died. Her words hit me like a truck, though. If we were expelled, we would be sent to the same BD school Zero had been sent to when he had gotten expelled, and I didn't want any of us to have to go there. All day, the three of us sat quietly in L.A.C., which was abnormal, considering she normally had to constantly remind us not to talk to each other. I assumed by the concerned looks on their faces that the others were also both thinking about what Ms. G had told us.

Fortunately for us, most of the BD teachers tried to be fair when giving out punishments, but the ones that weren't sent us to L.A.C. every chance they could get. It didn't take long for the in-school suspensions to turn into "out-of-schools," and they added up fast.

Before April was over, D and Ski Ski both exceeded ten out of school suspensions and were expelled from Sunnyslope High. I felt like it was my fault and that I deserved to be expelled as well. The only reason I hadn't been expelled yet was because of my counselor and one specific teacher.

Coach taught social studies in the BD hallway and was also the coach of the girl's soccer team. He had helped me throughout high school, constantly giving me second chances on late homework and allowing me to make up tests I missed when I ditched class. Every time I was about to fail, he was there to encourage me to succeed. My Ma, Sweetheart, and Coach were the only ones who hadn't given up on me graduating from high school yet, and half the reason I wanted to graduate was to make them proud and show them that believing in me wasn't a waste of their time and effort.

I wondered for hours if I should focus more on graduating first, then worry about the dealers after I graduated. Yet, I couldn't stop worrying that more kids could end up dead if I did that, and I wasn't going to let that happen. As anxious as I was about the consequences, I had to finish what I started. No matter what.

D's initial experience upon being sent to the BD school was similar to what happened with Zero. D didn't stay at the BD school long. He ended up dropping out after a few weeks, and fortunately, with the help and support of his friends and family, he was able to start working towards getting his GED. Furthermore, his mom got him a job at the local grocery store, and he started working part time there to pay for college. He absolutely hated working there, though, since he was a cashier and had to constantly deal with the stuck-up citizens from both sides of Sunnyslope.

All things considered, though, D was doing good for himself. He even went on to sign up for the community college and constantly bragged about the fact that he was going to sign up for college a few months sooner than the rest of the kids our age. This annoyed the hell out of a lot of the people who expected him to fail.

Ski Ski, on the other hand, decided to stay at the BD school so he could get his diploma, and he surprisingly seemed to fit in at the school very well. He even ended up making a few friends there. It seemed odd as to why he got along with the kids so well and fit in so easily, when both Zero and D didn't. However, I didn't give it too much thought, since he would only be there for a little bit, and it looked as if Ski Ski would go on to graduate. I thanked God that he wouldn't be stuck in the same situation as Zero.

While I was happy that everything seemed to be working out for my friends, I missed all my friends in the BD hallway. Thank God for Sweetheart. If it weren't for her, I would be lost at school, now that the rest of the Group had either graduated, dropped out, moved, or gotten expelled. My social anxiety made it so difficult to make new friends.

"Jason, if you get expelled. I am going to be so mad at you," said Sweetheart. She now spent most of her time trying to keep me from getting into trouble, which wasn't easy since the BD hallway felt like a ghost town now and the teachers, deans, hall monitors, and a lot of dealers still had it out for me. I was able to appreciate Sweetheart now, more than ever.

Sweetheart continued to try and help me stay out of trouble by helping me avoid as many hall monitors and teachers as possible.

"Get inside quick!" she said one time, and I jumped inside her locker to hide as she quickly slammed it shut. I heard my dean greet her as I remained in the locker.

At one point, I figured Sweetheart could write passes for me to get me out of class.

"Ski Ski gave me the booklet of passes that he stole from one of the teachers after he got expelled," I told her as she smiled and shook her head.

At first she refused.

"But now I don't have to receive any unexcused absences, and I won't get any more suspensions," I pressed her before she finally agreed.

"Fine, but you have to promise me that you won't ditch or be late for any more classes unless I give you a pass," she said.

"I promise," I told her, knowing that I wasn't gonna break that promise or any other to her, no matter what.

I missed Ms. G. I didn't typically go more than a week without at least having lunch with her. The good news though, was that it was almost May, and Sweetheart and I only had to lay low for a few more weeks before we graduated.

I had mixed feelings about graduation. While I was nervous about high school ending, I was also feeling accomplished. I had so many good memories over the past four years, while there were also a lot of things I had never had the chance to do. It wasn't just high school that was ending, but it was my childhood too. I was both excited and afraid of what was next. I didn't feel prepared for what came after.

I knew I wanted to be a firefighter. I had wanted to be one since I was in elementary school. They were real-life superheroes, and fire trucks reminded me of the Batmobile, with all their gadgets and tools. Still, it was scary to think about all that change. I had just finally gotten the hang of high school, and now it was about to be over. At the same time, I was relieved because I had been so stressed out about whether or not I would have enough credits to graduate, even if I did manage to avoid getting expelled.

The one good thing that had come out of all of the craziness of this year was that since Sweetheart and I were spending so much time together, just the two of us, we became even closer than we were before. She, of course, had to know I had had a crush on her since we met, and I think that she liked me too. What I didn't understand was that if she liked me, why couldn't she have made the first move to make it easier on me? I must have daydreamed about it a thousand times.

When I finally told her I wanted to be more than just friends, I didn't even plan for it. I saw her talking to one of the kids from the special education class, who had been sitting alone, and she quickly pulled out one of the birthday cards from the stack she kept in her purse. She always told me that she kept the stack on her because

"You never know when you'll run into someone and it's their birthday."

She signed the card and handed it to the kid, and his face lit up. The kid left shortly after receiving his card when it just came out.

"I love you" I told her instantly, surprised that I let it slip out.

"Did I say that out loud?" I followed up.

She looked at me and smiled. Then she grabbed my shirt to pull me in and kissed me. I was glad she interrupted me before I could try to take it back. I guess as soon as she thought I was finally going for it, she decided to make it easy on me. This was part of why I liked her so much, she almost always knew what I was thinking, and I didn't even have to say it. We were surprisingly very similar, other than the fact that she had always been a very social girl from the Southside, and she usually followed the rules. I was happier than ever now that I was finally in a relationship for the first time in my life, and it was with one of my best friends.

She later admitted to me that she was waiting for me to make the first move.

"I didn't want to make you uncomfortable and anxious around me," she said. Unfortunately, I was usually too anxious to tell her, and I didn't want to risk getting rejected and losing her.

Things went well once Sweetheart and I finally started dating. Except that I knew that we would have to hide it from her parents since they thought I was a drug dealer, thanks to the newspapers, after Jon, Ski Ski, and I got arrested.

The first and last time I went to Sweetheart's house was memorable.

"Um...I'm Ja..." I softly said, expecting Sweetheart to answer the door, surprised to see it was not.

I normally would have planned out the situation, but at the time, everything happened so fast that I didn't know what to do. Usually when I meet someone that I wanna make a good impression on, I like it to be as private as possible. The first thing I do is give them a heads up that I have social anxiety disorder so that they are patient with me and don't think that I'm being short or acting uninterested in what they are saying.

Her father, however, interrupted me after her mother gave me a dirty look and said,

"I better not see you near my daughter again." Then he shut the door in my face. Just being a BD kid with a skateboard from a low-income family in the Northside was bad enough, but now most of the town thought me and my family and friends were the ones selling drugs and attacking people who say no.

"My parents asked if I still talk to you, after hearing about you being arrested for selling drugs," Sweetheart said sadly, getting me out of my head and back to the present. We were standing outside her house.

I looked at her in shock.

"They told me that I better not be friends with you still. So, if they find out we started dating, they'll freak out and send me off to college as soon as we graduate. But no one is gonna stop me from seeing you," she finished.

I smiled at her. Thankfully my little rebel didn't listen, but if they found out we started dating it would create even more problems for us. So we decided to keep it a secret.

"It looks like we're gonna have to find a place where we can meet where no adults can find us," said Sweetheart

"What about the Lookout?" I suggested.

"That works for when we're outside of school. What about in school? Someone will eventually tell my parents," said Sweetheart

"The Ditch Door," I responded

"What's the Ditch Door?" asked Sweetheart, confused

"That's right. You don't know because you're a weirdo who's never ditched class," I joked.

"The Ditch Door is a stairway that goes from the second floor down to the first, but it only leads outside instead of connecting to the rest of the first floor. It was originally for seniors who are allowed off-campus, but now seniors have to use the main entrance. So it's always empty. I've been using it since freshman year," I casually confessed to her.

"Of course you have." Sweetheart seemed amused.

"So it's a door to nowhere basically." she added.

"Yeah, the hall monitor will occasionally look down there to make sure no one is ditching, but when we hear someone coming downstairs, we can just hide under the stairwell."

"Where is it?" she asked

"It's in the back of the school," I responded

"Okay, that sounds perfect. I better get back inside now before my parents wake up. I'll see you at the Ditch Door tomorrow…You're starting to rub off on me," she said with a smile before walking away.

"Now you know how it feels," I yelled over my shoulder, heading in the other direction.

From then on, the two of us met by the Ditch Door every day to go off campus and have lunch together at the park next to the skate park. The Ditch Door also became our hideout when we needed to get away from everyone or just wanted to see each other while at school. We met up every chance we got to spend every second we could together, even if it was just for a few minutes in between classes. Sweetheart only had to write us both passes excusing us for being late to prevent any unnecessary L.A.C. visits or suspensions.

I sometimes felt uncomfortable with how happy I was. I started to see how people could actually enjoy life. It wasn't just being with Sweetheart ,but it was also the progress that was being made with the drug problem. My anxiety and depression weren't that bad for the first time in as long as I could remember.

One day, Coach interrupted me as I was about to give him a pass that Sweetheart had written for me

"Are you ready to head down to the dean's office for your meeting?"

"What meeting?" I asked, confused and breaking eye contact. My mind had been on nothing but Sweetheart.

"Your yearly meeting with your parents and all of your teachers. Remember? I told you about it last week." Coach didn't look surprised that I had forgotten. After all, I rarely remembered to do my homework or bring a pencil to his class.

"Oh yeah, I forgot all about that. Can I go to the bathroom first? Then I'll meet you guys down there?" I needed to let Sweetheart know that I couldn't make it to see her.

"No, my friend, I want you to walk down there with me, so I can make sure you come and aren't late," Coach said. He smiled so respectfully that I couldn't respond with anything other than,

"Okay."

I was disappointed. Alone time with Sweetheart by the Ditch Door was the best part of my day. I actually looked forward to going to school now. I pulled out my phone and texted her to let her know what was going on. I knew I shouldn't be mad at Coach, but I couldn't help it, since he unintentionally ruined all of that excitement and happiness that had filled me just a few minutes prior to running into him.

A few minutes later, I walked into the meeting, and there, sitting around a table, were all of my teachers, my dean, and my counselor, who was talking to my Ma. My dean started talking.

"Now that Jason has ten out-of-school suspensions. I think that it's time we discuss his future at another school."

I felt a sharp pain in my stomach as I sunk in my seat. I could've sworn that Coach told me that I only had nine. My Ma gave me dirty looks, while most of my teachers and my counselor looked surprised. My dean continued,

"He'll be expelled... He'll be going to the BD school... I'm sure he won't mind since he'll be reunited with a few of his friends."

I only heard bits and pieces of what he was saying as I began to have an anxiety attack. I struggled to breathe and felt like running out of the meeting, thinking about all of the problems I was gonna face going forward. I wished I was with Sweetheart somewhere, away from everyone else. I needed her. Only she could make everything feel okay again. Sweetheart and I had just started dating.

What if we broke up because we wouldn't be able to see each other at school anymore?

I was about to ask to go to the bathroom so that I could go find her when Coach, shuffling papers and wearing a look equally as confused as mine, interrupted me.

"Excuse me, but according to my notes, it says that Jason only has nine out of school suspensions. Has he been suspended between then and now?"

I felt a glimpse of hope.

"Um... let me check again. Oh, well I must have miscounted," said my dean, clearly trying to hide his frustration.

I felt instant relief.

"Although," my dean continued,

"To be honest, I think any day now he will get suspended since, he's always getting into trouble. So we should do us all a favor and just go ahead and discuss it while we are all here," he added, making his intentions clear.

"If he gets another one, then we'll discuss it," said my Ma, clearly frustrated. I imagined she was probably almost as worried as I was.

Coach weighed in,

"I agree. Jason hasn't gotten into any trouble or had any unexcused absences in almost two weeks, which is his longest streak yet. Personally, I wanna see how long he can keep this going for. It took until the last month of high school, but he's finally doing it." Most of us in the meeting laughed.

"That's because his only friends here have all been expelled," my dean replied.

Still, I felt like the others in the meeting were starting to take my side.

"Even so," Coach said,

"The school year ends next month. If he can go just another two weeks without getting into trouble, catch up on all of his missing assignments and pass all of his classes, he will have exactly forty-four and a half credits, and he will be able to graduate. He's been trying to do better both in and out of school. Don't you think we should at least give him a chance to succeed before sending him to a school where he doesn't belong and where we all know he will fail?" Me and my Ma waited anxiously for a response.

121

Chapter 6

Organized Crime Fighting

All my overwhelming anxiety was gone in a flash. After all of my teachers and my guidance counselor took turns weighing in, it was decided that I would be able to finish my senior year at Sunnyslope High as long as I didn't get another out-of-school suspension. It mostly had to do with both Coach and my counselor speaking up on behalf of my staying. I was so grateful that I just happened to have the two of them in charge of whether or not I'd go to the BD school.

I knew I would never forget the people who helped me throughout my life. All the teachers and counselors and anyone who gave me extra time on my work because they knew I struggled with a lot of issues. Or the people who looked out for me even when I was misbehaving because they knew I tried to be better. My dean looked so much like he was trying to keep his cool that I couldn't help but lose mine and smile. Thank God that unless I got my tenth suspension, there was nothing he could do.

The last month of school flew by in what felt like a montage. I was at times happier and at times sadder and more anxious than I had ever been before. Sweetheart helped me as I scrambled to finish all of my missing assignments and make up all of the tests I hadn't taken.

The rest of the seniors, the ones who had worked hard for three and a half years, got to slack off the last semester. Meanwhile, I had slacked off for three and a half years and now had to work as hard as I could to catch up.

Sweetheart admitted to me that she actually had enough credits to graduate early if she wanted to. However, she decided to stay and finish out the school year with me. She would've graduated back when Chish moved. I couldn't have been more thankful for her choosing to stay with me. I don't know what I would've done without her.

As a fortunate twist, all the times I had been put in L.A.C. throughout the year had given me the time to make up for a lot of my missing work. So catching up on everything was possible. I walked on eggshells for the rest of the year by thinking about every possible outcome of every decision I made and choosing every word and action carefully.

I passed all of my senior finals. Then on May 16th at one-thirteen p.m, my counselor showed me the note she had received from Coach. She had pinned it to the bulletin board in her office. I read the note, which said, "Jason is graduating." I smiled.

To the surprise of everyone, I had passed all of my classes and had just enough credits to graduate from high school. I was too anxious to celebrate in front of my counselor, so I remained stoic until I left her office and then went and told Sweetheart.

It was hard for me to keep my emotions in check as I said goodbye to Coach, Ms. G, my counselor, and Sunnyslope High altogether. Some parts of graduation were difficult, especially the severe anxiety that came with being around a crowded gymnasium during the graduation ceremony, even more so while I walked across the stage. Yet, I also felt proud of myself and thankful for all the help I got from my family, friends, teachers, Sweetheart, Coach, and everyone else who had been there for me.

I can't believe I did it, and I can't believe it's over. I'm actually gonna miss it, I said to myself as I thought about my childhood. I couldn't believe how much had happened in that year alone. I thought about Zero and all the battles we encountered with the dealers. I looked around the school for the last time, part of me afraid to leave and move on since I didn't know what was next. That was until Sweetheart grabbed my hand and led me towards the door, and we walked out of the building for the last time together. I felt I could do anything as long as I had her.

After the graduation ceremony, both my mom and dad gave me a hug.

"I'm proud of you," each one of them told me. It was always weird whenever we were all together. They split up right after Jeff was born so it was hard to even imagine us being like other families.

Jon and Jeff didn't hug me, thankfully, and instead both gave me the finger. Jon, then later Jeff, said,

"Good job, bitch." These were always our words of support.

I got a chance to secretly kiss and say goodbye to Sweetheart before she went out to dinner with her parents. Then the rest of the Group and I went to celebrate by going to our usual skate spots around town. Even Chish made it out after graduating from his new school on the same day.

I was shocked that Ski Ski was able to graduate with me from Sunnyslope High instead of the BD school. I laughed to myself when I thought about how out of all my friends, other than Sweetheart, *he* was the only one to graduate with me. I was really excited. All my friends and my brothers had made it out, and I was able to hangout with all of them for the first time in a while and have some well-deserved fun.

We had to avoid the cops out patrolling and with the occasional car that sped past filled with either North or Southsiders that would yell something at us. By then, though, we were used to it.

"Skater bitches!" they yelled. One of us, usually Jeff or Ski Ski, would just yell back.

Or Anthony would run after the car.

"Get out of your car and say that to our face!" Of course, they never did. As we skated uptown, I was still thinking about the fact that I had just graduated high school.

That was until Ski Ski interrupted my train of thought.

"I forgot to mention that while I was in jail, I talked to a few guys who knew who Chronic was. I guess he supplied them with drugs to sell in the town they lived in."

"Really?" I asked, surprised.

"Yeah, I just got a text from one of the guys who was in there with me. He said that Chronic is Uptown. He's at Smokers Alley selling to someone right now." Surprised, we all looked at one another.

"Let's go get him," Jon responded immediately. I could tell that Jon was most likely thinking the same thing I was. If we stopped Chronic now, the other dealers wouldn't be able to get their hands on any more drugs to sell.

We all agreed to head towards Smokers Alley to finally find Zero's dealer. We experienced a mixture of emotions as we made our way Uptown. We felt both anger and excitement as we eagerly got closer and closer to finally seeing this guy face to face. This was the moment we all had been waiting for.

"Graduating and stopping Chronic in the same night sounds like a great way to start off the summer and wrap up the school year," I said to Ski Ski. He grinned and nodded up and down at me in return.

When we reached the alleyway, we walked between the two large buildings that blocked out almost all light only to find it empty.

We all turned to Ski Ski, and I asked,

"What's going on?"

"Where is he?" Jon said.

"No one's here," Jeff added.

We all looked around, confused, as Ski Ski shrugged.

"He's supposed to be here."

"Behind us," said Anthony, and he pointed to the entrance of the alley from where we had come in, which was now blocked by what looked like around a dozen guys, give or take.

I instinctively tried to count to see if the odds were stacked against us or in our favor. We quickly recognized the dealers we had fought before. It looked as if the Northside and Southside dealers had decided to work together and somehow manage to set us up. I surveyed the dealers, hoping there would be one I wouldn't recognize, someone who could be Chronic, but unfortunately, I had seen all of them before, and none of them were Chronic.

"How did they know that we would be here?" Jeff asked. Jon and I looked at each other, then at Ski Ski suspiciously.

"We'll figure that out later. Right now we have to deal with them," I said.

Jon and I didn't have time to argue about how to handle the situation, so we played a round of rock, paper, scissors for a quick decision about who would take the lead on the situation, which came as a surprise to both groups. If I had won, we would've just attacked them, but Jon won, and I knew he would try to reason with the dealers first. The two of us walked ahead and approached the dealers. Jon looked back and, sure enough, said to the others,

"You guys stay here while I talk to them."

"Jeff, no matter what happens stay out of it," I added, walking with Jon. Jeff exhaled, annoyed.

As we approached the dealers, Jon looked at one of them, who I recognized as one of his classmates from back when he was in high school.

"We don't have to do this," Jon pleaded with them.

"Just stop selling drugs and we can all go our separate ways. No one else has to get hurt."

The dealers, smirks on their faces, looked at Jon, and one of them, who also looked about his age, said,

"They chose to buy from us. It's not our fault they're all stupid enough to take the stuff."

From his face, I could tell Jon was as furious as I was.

"You're giving heroin to desperate kids who are struggling and telling them that it's cocaine," Jon said to the dealer, looking even more enraged.

I assumed he was also thinking about Zero.

"We don't make any of them…" one of the dealers began, and I suddenly had an image of Zero laying in his bed taking his last breath.

"Quiet. Give us your supply, then tell us where Chronic is now!" I yelled at the top of my lungs, clenching my fists. I felt Jon turn and look at me. A small part of me that I felt growing smaller by the second fought to try and remind me of who I was.

The dealers started talking quietly amongst themselves, appearing to be planning something,

"Are you ready?" Jon asked me.

"Yeah," I answered. We both raised our fists and put our guard up, fearing the dealers were just going to charge at us. Then the dealers attacked, all of them charging us together. Right as they collided with Jon and me, the rest of the BD kids came behind us to back us up, and a huge brawl broke out between the two groups.

We were holding our own, despite being so caught off guard from the start. I heard shouting all around me right before it was slowly silenced by the sound of the rain that started pouring down on everyone. It became obvious to me who would win since one side had something worth fighting for.

The only one not actively fighting at this point was Jeff, but despite what I had told him, Jeff, as usual, didn't listen and didn't stay out of it for long. While our Group fought the dealers, Jeff made his way throughout the alley to lend a hand to anyone that was struggling in the fight. He just started kicking or punching any dealers that looked as if they had an upper hand on one of us. Even if his attacks weren't enough to stop them, he did provide a necessary distraction to give our side the advantage in the fight. Since the dealers were forced to use their hands to cover their bodies as Jeff hit them, they left themselves open for us to get in some headshots.

The rain continued, and the fight didn't last much longer, as the dealers began to retreat one by one. Some looked absolutely furious and others scared as they fled. I looked around as cheers rang out from some of my friends in celebration of our victory, while others were slow to get up. Jon's nose appeared to be broken, my eye was throbbing, and it was clear that Chish needed to go to the hospital. He could barely stand.

I surveyed my friends, That's when I realized I was wrong. I had wanted to prevent anyone else from becoming a drug addict. I had wanted to redeem myself for the bad friend I had been to Zero. To try and make his death mean something. I didn't want the rest of my friends or my family to get hurt or outcast by the whole town in the process. I was even more pissed off when I realized that Ski Ski was missing.

He must have gotten afraid and took off as we were fighting. I was unsurprised. He had done that before.

He's lucky I made that promise to Zero. Why else would I still hang out with him? I thought as I helped

Chish who was struggling to move, and suddenly I had a soul crushing revelation.

I did the same thing as everybody else. I pretended that everyone else but my group was the problem.

I left to take Chish to the Sunnyslope hospital, and everyone planned to head back to the Lookout. The younger members of the Group were still cheering and high-fiving as we were leaving.

As I sat in the waiting room of the hospital waiting to hear about how Chish was doing, deep in thought about everything that had happened this year, I finally started to understand why my friends didn't agree from the start. I had to find another way to do my part and help with the drug problem. Things usually got worse before they got better, and I had assumed that all the things that happened this year were things in town getting worse before they got better. This is why it was so easy to confuse escalation with progress. It was so obvious to me now.

"How's Chish?" said Jon as I walked up the porch of the Lookout a few hours later.

"The Doc said he'll be fine. He just has a concussion. I had to take him home to get some rest. He couldn't take the train in his condition."

"Good," Jon replied

"You guys were right," I said to Jon and Sweetheart, who had just walked outside. A half-angry, half worried expression came across her face when she saw my black eye. "Attacking them made it worse. The whole town is after us because they think we're the ones selling drugs, and now my friends are getting hurt because of me."

"What are you talking about? That was awesome. We won," Jeff said cheerfully.

"Jeff, our friends got hurt. Things have gotten worse. I handled it wrong." Ashamed of myself, I stared at the ground.

I tried to help, but now I don't know what's me and what's an intrusive thought anymore. I'm the monster who doesn't realize that he is the bad guy, I thought to myself, realizing that you can be a good person trying to stand up for what's right, and in a blink of an eye you quickly become the villain without even realizing it.

I felt a sharp pain of regret when I thought about Sarge, who had stopped responding to us after the brawl in Smokers Alley. We never found out why Sarge had just disappeared after the fight was over, but I assumed it was because he was afraid that if we had continued fighting and getting in trouble we would all end up in jail like Ski Ski did, a fear I also always had, given my family history. Coming from a family of gangsters and substance abusers was one of the main causes of my many mental illnesses. Jon, Jeff, and I all tried to break that cycle, but if we weren't careful we would all end up in jail and ruin the new path our grandfather had created for us when he found Jesus and devoted his life to helping people rather than hurting them.

"Some stuff has gotten worse, but some things have gotten better," Jon said, interrupting my thoughts.

"I was wrong too. We can't just wait for someone to become an addict and then decide to do something. We need to find another way to handle this."

"I agree," I said

"I do too," Jeff added after listening to his older brothers for once, which came to a surprise to all three of us since rarely did we all agree on something. That's when Sweetheart casually mentioned an idea that was better than any of ours.

Chapter 7

Rise For The Fallen

"What if you guys just found the dealers and called Gordon to come and arrest them one by one? That way you only have to fight if you need to in self-defense." I listened to Sweetheart's suggestion as she examined my eye.

"He told us that he can't do it all by himself," I said to her.

"That was before. Things have gotten even worse since then. The whole town is freaking out. I think everybody just wants things to go back to normal. Sometimes things have to get worse before people are willing to compromise and make things better. I'll also try to figure out a way to get the real story out there."

Jon, Jeff, and I tried to read each other and then smiled in agreement. She was right! The next day me, Jon, and Jeff all met Gordon at Misfits to tell him about our new plan.

"I would ask what happened to all of your faces, but why pretend like I don't already know," said Gordon. The three of us started cracking up.

I explained Sweetheart's new plan to Gordon.

"Sweetheart pointed out that we could find the dealers and call you. Then we can intimidate them into staying put until you show up. She pointed out that things have gotten so bad that even the rich kids can't get away with it anymore."

"She's right. The police chief told us to arrest any dealers we find, no matter what they look like or what side of town they are from, though a lot of the officers are hesitant because they are friends with most of the rich kids' parents. But I agree with you guys. If this doesn't end soon, our town will plunge into anarchy. You guys are good kids. Call me when you find any dealers. Be careful out there though," Gordon finished before walking away.

After a few weeks of us working side by side with Gordon, most of the dealers in Sunnyslope had been arrested, and the ones who weren't were too afraid of going to jail or what we would do to them to keep selling. The rich kids' parents were able to get them out of trouble for a while, but after Gordon's arresting them multiple times, all the money in the world couldn't prevent them from going to jail, and my Ma managed to get a journalist to print an article on social media to acknowledge what was really happening.

Gordon had also inspired some of the other cops to do what's right. He said to us,

"I told them that right and wrong don't depend on who carries out the action. It's the action itself that makes you right or wrong, regardless of who you are or what you look like. Everyone deserves a second chance to be a better person, but until they are ready to change, anyone who victimizes others needs to be stopped as passively as possible. And the group of officers, well almost all of them, nodded their heads and smiled in agreement. I could tell they thought about what has happened to our town."

The overdoses drastically started decreasing in Sunnyslope, and we all felt like we had finally done it. We came to the realization that we couldn't save everyone, however, when the overdoses didn't stop completely, and after the dealers stopped selling in Sunnyslope, some of the addicts just started going to the city to get their drugs.

The I-290 East was the highway that took you to and from the city and suburbs of Chicago and was nicknamed Heroin Highway because a few of the exits off the highway took you right to where all the dealers in the city were. As much as we would've loved to put a stop to those dealers too, we knew that realistically there was only so much we could do to help. Not to mention Gordon's jurisdiction was only in Sunnyslope, and the number of crooked cops in Sunnyslope was nothing compared to the ones in the city.

As the overdoses continued to decrease, things slowly started to go back to normal in town. The prejudice against the BD kids never really went away on the North or Southside, and neither did the hatred between the lower and upper classes. We still dealt with people driving past and yelling stuff at us. We also still dealt with crooked cops. We even still dealt with citizens who openly insulted us in front of the cops, knowing we couldn't do anything about it, and we still occasionally got into fights. However, now we only fought to defend ourselves.

The only time everyone was able to agree on anything was when they found a common enemy in the BD kids. It didn't matter to us though. We finally saw that we made a difference in town, even if none of them appreciated it.

Things got even better in town when one after another the mayor, principal, and police chief all chose to resign. In a twist of events, it seemed that blaming the troubled youths with behavioral issues was a double-edged sword. The town's leaders lost all credibility when it turned out that the BD kids weren't the ones selling drugs after all. Sweetheart even convinced her parents to give me another chance after they found out that it was my Ma who helped her to get the real story of what was happening out there.

Sweetheart took me to meet her parents again as a chance to start fresh.

"Hi," I basically mumbled as I shook both her parents' hands, extremely nervous and socially anxious. I was hoping I wouldn't mess up my second chance. At first I forgot to smile, and I broke eye contact, I was so nervous. I was worried I might come across as disrespectful. As a little time went by, though, I finally got more comfortable around them and was able to be myself. They even apologized for judging me. I was thrilled when they seemed like they maybe even liked me a little.

"I get why you like him," Sweetheart's mother said. I think she thought I was out of earshot.

"Why is that?" asked Sweetheart.

"Because he's the male version of you," her mom said. Sweetheart and both of her parents laughed as I secretly grinned.

Though it seemed as if it was all over, we knew it wasn't. The Group still had one more thing to take care of: finding Chronic. It looked like he had moved on to another town, as we hadn't heard anything about him, and I couldn't imagine that he also had a change of heart like I did.

He has to be just staying out of Sunnyslope until he thinks things calm down, I thought to myself. After all, the dealers had either given up selling or were arrested and finally charged, but I had hoped that we would run into him eventually.

Throughout the rest of May and June, I looked into a fire fighting program at the local college near the school Sweetheart had been accepted to. I naturally assumed I wouldn't get into her school.

"I doubt your new school has a BD program," I said to Sweetheart, and we both laughed.

In the meantime, the Group still hadn't heard anything about Chronic or whether or not he'd been in Sunnyslope. While some of my friends started to think that we may never find him, I didn't give up hope.

"It's over man. He's not coming back," said D.

"Yeah, I think D's right, Jay. He knows if we catch him he's screwed. He'll get hurt, go to jail, or both. Even if we don't find him. It doesn't matter as long as he can't sell to anybody anymore." Chish said.

Still, I asked Colin to continue to put the word out talk to everyone around town, and wait for someone to come forward and tell us anything about where he was. We still, at this point, surprisingly hadn't seen what he looked like. It was challenging for us to accept that a lot of people choose not to do the right thing, and it's not always because they fear what will happen if they do. Some people genuinely believe that trying to stop someone who's done something wrong is worse than the person who's doing something wrong.

Chicago is one of those cities where criminals have a good chance of getting away with crimes, mainly because those who witness the crime refuse to do the right thing. Being a "snitch" is somehow considered worse than being a criminal, which is ironic since only criminals can snitch. I learned that a snitch is a criminal who provides info on other criminals for the purpose of getting themselves out of the consequences of their actions. A person who reports someone for selling drugs or victimizing somebody without expecting anything in return is doing the right thing. Most people lack the honor, though, which is both the courage and the integrity it takes to do what is right.

On the Fourth of July, all the BD kids decided to have a bonfire and barbecue in the backyard of the Lookout to celebrate the decrease in overdoses. All of the internal conflicts I had been struggling with about whether or not I had been doing the right thing were in the past, now that we had a new passive and more effective approach to handling the problem.

I could tell it wasn't just me either. With every dealer arrest, my family and friends all seemed a lot happier and more at peace. I felt so much relief, like all of this was worth it now. For a while, I had just felt like I was selfishly causing problems to make up for being a bad friend to Zero. Now I felt like we were able to turn things around before it was too late and find an opportunity in all of the chaos.

It was way too hot to hang out inside. The AC wasn't turned on, as no one was supposed to be living there. Everybody met up and pitched in for some drinks, food, and a bunch of other necessities for a barbecue. While the others were busy setting up, Anthony and I took a ride to the grocery store.

Upon returning, Jon told me that while we were out Colin had revealed to Jon a sad truth he had learned. After months of him constantly asking around about Chronic, he finally found out information about another dealer. It turned out that one of the BD kids had been selling drugs the entire time we were on our mission. I didn't want to believe the news. We had lived in denial for a long time. At the same time, I wasn't surprised, given who it was. For now, I needed to act as if everything was normal until we could discuss how to handle it privately, even though it was killing me on the inside.

That Saturday, July 7th, was Zero's birthday. My brothers, my Ma, and I visited Zero's grave that day. Other than that, the day started like any other day. Then I got a phone call from Ski Ski.

"Dude I found him!" he screamed into the phone with excitement.

"Who?" I asked, emotionally drained after visiting the cemetery, not even wanting to hear Ski Ski's voice.

"Chronic. He's at the Forest Preserve right now. One of the guys from the BD School is selling for him in another neighborhood. He told me that Chronic is at the Forest Preserve now, waiting for one of his dealers to deliver something," Ski Ski once again eagerly informed me.

"Okay, I'll start calling everyone so we can all…" I was getting a little excited at the opportunity to find Chronic.

Ski Ski interrupted me,

"Nooo!…he won't be there long. I'm almost there. Me, you, and Jon can handle him ourselves. Go tell Jon, and meet me on the bridge by the creek. We will get him together."

"Alright, me and Jon will be there soon," I told him. It had taken me a while to master seeing through his lies and knowing when he was trying to manipulate me. Since he was so good at faking emotions, and since I also had a tendency to idealize the people that I cared about, I could now tell what he was doing, even if it was over the phone.

"Alright cool, I'll see you guys th…" Ski Ski said as I hung up my phone before he could even finish his sentence.

I told Jon everything, and we headed to the Forest Preserve to meet one of our oldest friends. When we got there, we found Ski Ski waiting for us on the bridge, seemingly texting someone. When he approached us, he shook our hands and hugged us to say hello before we headed in, ready to end this once and for all. Ski Ski was unusually hyped up, to the point that it was obvious that he wasn't sincere. I felt more down than usual, and Jon was noticeably more sad too.

"Why do you guys look so sad? This is what we've been waiting for. We're finally gonna get him," said Ski Ski

"I'm always brooding. And on top of that, we were just at Zero's grave," I said, hoping it would affect Ski Ski in any way, but it didn't.

"Well we can all be happy because we're getting revenge for Zero right now, and then all of this will be over," said Ski Ski.

"We'll get justice, not revenge," I quickly pointed out.

"There's a difference."

"Then it will all be over," Jon added

"Yeah. That's what I meant." Ski Ski quickly finished.

As the three of us got down to the creek, we immediately spotted Chronic. Rage immediately filled Jon and I as we placed our eyes on him for the first time. He looked like a stereotypical drug dealer, with baggy clothes, a crooked Sox hat, and tattoos covering his body and face. You could tell just by looking at him that he was one of those guys who thought he was a gangster. Unfortunately for him, Jon and I had met a real gangster and knew the difference. We weren't intimidated.

"So you guys are the snitches my dealers have been so afraid of. You look soft to me," said Chronic as he walked towards the three of us, also seemingly enraged.

Despite everything that happened, we struggled with whether or not we should just start hitting him.

"Maybe we can just beat the hell out of both of them, and just say they tried to run," I said to Jon.

"This is Chronic. If anyone deserves it, it's him," Jon replied.

"Why don't you guys speak up so I can hear you?" said Chronic loudly.

"Mind your business, you poorly raised little bitch," I snapped at him.

143

He smiled and said,

"Thanks for bringing them here, Ski Ski. This makes us even for the money you owe me."

Jon and I looked at Ski Ski in disappointment. Who looked down, pretended to be ashamed, and walked over to stand by Chronic's side. Chronic started pulling up his pants, indicating that there was about to be a fight. I couldn't even tell if Ski Ski felt guilty or felt anything at all.

"He's been selling for me at his school for months," Chronic told us.

"One of your friends. This whole time. When I finally found out he was your friend, I figured out how I could get you guys alone." A disgusting grin still stretched across his ugly face.

"We know," said Jon. Chronic and Ski Ski both looked shocked by this revelation.

"We found out a few days ago, on the Fourth of July," Jon finished

"We always knew you were a scumbag, but we thought that maybe you could become a better person if we showed you how. We were wrong." I looked at one of my now ex-best friends with revulsion.

"You don't get how hard it is to get a job with a record. And I have to pay a lot of fines from when we got arrested," Ski Ski whined.

"Oh shut the hell up!" I yelled in a response so loud I heard my voice echo throughout the forest.

Jon said,

"There are places that will hire people with a criminal record as long as you act civilized. You just think you're too good to work at those places. We could've helped you try to find a way to get money to pay your fines. You could've come and worked at our gym to save up money. Instead, after what he did to Zero, your friend, you helped him." Jon pointed his finger toward Chronic.

He went on, now almost yelling,

"What, is selling heroin to teenagers cooler than working at a fast-food restaurant or teaching kids how to box?" I asked.

"You're lying to everyone about what they are taking. Nothing justifies that."

"You guys caught on to that, did you?" said Chronic with another hideous grin as Jon went to charge him.

Yet, in an ironic twist, I tried to stop him.

"Wait Jon," I said as I got in front of him.

He stopped.

"If they attack us, we'll defend ourselves." I spoke softly to Jon so that only he could hear. I could tell Jon was starting to lose control. After everything we had just heard and everything that had happened, being face to face with Zero's dealer was hard to handle calmly, especially since he clearly showed no remorse for the things he had done. Or had any intentions of stopping what he was doing.

"I told you, Ski Ski, there's no such thing as right or wrong. It's survival of the fittest. People with power and money survive, and the weak don't," said Chronic.

"Your parents really did a number on you, didn't they? And I thought that I was the monster," I said, looking at him with an involuntary expression of judgment.

"That's enough talking," said Chronic to Ski Ski.

"It's their turn to get hurt. Let's get 'em."

Ski Ski looked visibly afraid.

"What are you scared of? I'm not gonna hurt you," Chronic chided Ski Ski.

"It's not you that he's afraid of," said Jon as both of us quickly put our guards up to get ready to defend ourselves.

Just as the fight was about to start, we all heard a loud, familiar, and deep voice yelled,

"Where's my bitch?!?"

The four of us all stopped and turned towards the entrance of the forest to see Anthony followed by Colin, Chish, D, Andy, and Jeff. Chronic's face became just as visibly shaken as Ski Ski's.

"I told Jeff he shouldn't come with, but he followed us anyway," said Andy

"Don't worry about it, he doesn't listen to us either," said Jon.

"So this is my bitch." Anthony walked directly up to Chronic and Ski Ski without bluffing.

"I'll fight both of you at the same time. Let's Go."

The Group surrounded Chronic and Ski Ski, ready to attack, and I looked at every one of my friends and then at Jeff. Then I thought about Sweetheart, and I thought about Zero.

"Let's beat the hell out of both of them guys," said Jeff.

"No, don't!" I responded.

"Why? They deserve it!" said Jeff.

I was struggling to do what was right. I turned to Jon and said,

"Call Gordon, and we'll make sure neither of them goes anywhere until he gets here."

Jon slowly pulled out his phone, while not taking his eyes off Chronic, making it obvious that he really wanted to fight him.

"You think we're just gonna wait here for the cops to show up?" said Chronic

"You can try to leave if you want, but it's gonna hurt," I told Chronic. Then I said to my friends,

"If either of them tries to run, then you guys can do whatever you want to them." They all smiled and nodded to me.

"He's on his way," Jon confirmed a few minutes later, after getting off the phone with Gordon.

"Good," I replied, feeling the weight I had felt since October 2nd start to lift.

The rest of the group sat in the Forest Preserve, staring at Ski Ski and Chronic as they hoped and waited for one of them to try to make a move.

"Come on guys. Please? At least try to run," said Colin.

"It'll be a lot more fun than watching you get arrested.

"I'll give you a one-minute head start," Anthony followed up.

"Let's make a run for it. We can take all of them anyways. Just a bunch of spoiled kids from the suburbs," said Chronic quietly to Ski Ski.

Ski Ski educated Chronic as to who he was dealing with.

"Jon and Jay alone would've easily handled both of us. The rest showed up not because they didn't think they'd win, but because they figured we're not stupid enough to fight all of them. You do what you want, but we're not gonna be safe until the cops show up." Ski Ski went on,

"There's a reason I didn't want them finding out. I told you not to mess with them. I thought you had backup? More dealers?"

"They never showed," said Chronic

"I shouldn't have either," Ski Ski said.

"Stop talking or I'll start punching," said Anthony as a final warning.

Despite being encouraged to try and run, neither Chronic nor Ski Ski bothered trying to leave. Gordon showed up shortly after and arrested both of them.

"A lot of grieving families and friends are gonna finally get justice, thanks to you guys. I'm proud of all of you," said Gordon to the remaining members of the Group after putting both Chronic and Ski Ski in the back of his cop car.

Once they both were finally in the cop car, Chronic and Ski Ski apparently felt safe enough to start making threats and insulting us.

"This ain't over. I thought you guys were my friends. You were like brothers to me," said Ski Ski, shaking his head at us.

"Snitches! You won't fight me without your boys around. We'll find you. Just watch," said Chronic, though no one in the Group cared about what they were saying. We didn't even look at them. We just laughed at the muffled threats because it was finally over.

It was at that moment that I realized that innocence is the price of wisdom and that strength is measured by how gentle, sweet, charitable, sensitive, and optimistic you can remain in a world that forces you to be violent, bitter, selfish, hateful and pessimistic.

I guess maybe most people aren't as good as they pretend to be. And maybe I'm not as different as I think I am. For some people, life is about finding who you are or inventing who you are, but when it comes to good people, then life is about the struggle of staying who you are in a world that wants to change you. There's a fine line between progress and escalation, and justice and revenge.

It took a while, and it was a painful lesson, but I finally realized that life isn't a superhero movie. There's not a right side versus a wrong side. There are two wrong sides that take turns being right, and you have to adapt to the situation or you'll end up siding with the bad guys. Heroes, people who do the right thing for selfless reasons, do exist. So do villains, people who do the wrong thing for selfish reasons. Yet, most people are anti-heroes, people who do the right thing for selfish reasons or are anti-villains those who do the wrong thing for selfless reasons.

I finally accepted Zero's death, and even though I will always regret what I had done to him, I was able to forgive myself for how I treated my brother. Me and the rest of The Behavioral Disordered could breathe a sigh of relief as we watched Gordon drive off towards the police station with Chronic and Ski Ski, knowing that as long as we were smart, continued to do the right thing, and worked with him to stop any dealers, we could keep trying to prevent anyone else from using or selling drugs in our town again.